SNATCHING HILLARY

A Satirical Novel

by

Dick Carlson

and

Bill Cowan

Tulip Hill Publishers

www.SnatchingHillary.com

1

This is a work of fiction: political parody and satire. Names, characters, businesses, places and events are the product of the authors' imaginations or used in a fictitious manner.

References to real people, events, establishments, organizations or locales, and particularly to public figures, are intended to provide a sense of authenticity and are based on a fair evaluation of previously published material about their public and private lives.

"I hate this f'ing book as much as Hillary does!"

Bill Press, talk show host, liberal commentator, author and former chairman of the California Democrat Party.

"Funny, brilliant and incredibly creative. The authors skewer dozens of annoying politicians who haunt the Washington scene. This is a must read for those who desperately seek the good old days when both sides of the aisle overcame their differences with a sense of humor."

Dick Capen, former Publisher of the Miami Herald, former U.S. Ambassador to Spain.

*Dedicated to our families and friends
and to all who will find the humor
intended in this story.*

Introduction

"Like the moon, she shows us the same face each time we see her. Sometimes she displays more, sometimes less of her visage, but always it is the same carefully presented persona: friendly, open, giggly, practical, family-oriented, caring, thoughtful, unflappable, serious, balanced and moderate. Just like the moon, though, Hillary Rodham Clinton has a face she never shows us, a side that is never visible, never on display."

Dick Morris, Clinton political advisor.

Hillary Clinton is the front-running Democrat for her party's 2016 presidential nomination. It is a position she has held since Obama's 2012 election. Despite the bumps and bruises of the campaign, Hillary is poised for victory.

Every poll shows her to be the likely winner of the general election for the Presidency - something she's coveted since she and Bill left the White House in 2001.

Since her days at Wellesley and then at Yale, Hillary Clinton has been a hard and humorless worker, particularly when she was chasing something she desperately wanted.

Now, exhibiting the grit and determination she has developed over decades as other women built their glutes and abs or cooking and gardening skills, she's running hard for the Democratic nomination.

A few weeks before the New Hampshire primary, scheduled for mid-February, 2016, her campaign is beginning to stumble, and her popularity has slipped. The opposition, both inside and outside her own party, is sniping at her relentlessly and it's showing in the numbers. She can't seem to catch a break.

Her opponents in the primary, although all trailing by significant margins, are rising in the polls slowly and more steadily than expected.

Elizabeth Warren, age 66, the liberal doyenne, leads the pack despite compelling evidence she isn't at all the Indian she had claimed to be in the application that had gotten her onto the faculty at Harvard.

Vice President Joe Biden, age 74, the standard bearer for elderly Democrats and representative of millions of slightly befuddled Americans, hasn't been much hurt by his frequent lapses into momentary idiocy - he famously delivered an order to a Missouri politician, a former state senator named Charles Graham, a life-long paraplegic in a wheelchair whom Biden was pretending to know. Looking down from a stage at Graham, seated in the front row, Biden yelled, "Hey Chuck, get up and wave to the crowd."

Or by onetime CIA director and former Secretary of Defense Bob Gates' public remark that Biden has "been wrong on just about every foreign policy and national security issue over the past four decades." While his numbers have trailed Hillary's miserably, he has nothing to lose by a final run at the presidency.

California governor Jerry Brown, aged 78, smart and as devious as a ferret, with a record of erratic statements and oddball behavior, plus a few serious secrets tucked in the back of his closet under a pair of gold Chanel pumps, has announced his candidacy and is fighting hard against his "Governor Moonbeam" image and nickname. Jerry was reelected to a send four-year term in 2014, defeating his Republican opponent. In the summer primary. Brown defeated 13 other candidates, including the former media darling and "antiwar Peace Mom" Cindy Sheehan, who ran as a "feminist socialist." After almost daily coverage during the Bush 43 years, the media now ignores Sheehan, likely from embarrassment.

Finally, there's Deval Patrick, 60, Barrack Obama's friend and former governor of Massachusetts, replaced by Republican Charlie Baker in January 2015. Patrick and Obama's past political victories were the work of the same political Svengali, David Axelrod. A late entry to the presidential race, Patrick remains popular with African Americans and race-conscious whites, all of them clamoring for a second black man in the Oval Office. A "*real* black man, not a fifty per center," says radio host Joe Madison.

Tired but undaunted, Hillary presses on. Still, though the prize appears ready to drop into her kit bag, she needs to go through many motions, winning state primaries and wooing voters prime among them. For a candidate riding high on an endless wave of celebrity-popularity, it seems easy. But it is not.

Shortly before the New Hampshire primary her security detail stumbles. She is kidnapped from a Washington, D.C., fundraiser. The world turns upside down.

Chapter One

In Washington, D.C., in Georgetown, at a large imposing house on N Street, Hillary is preparing to speak at a $10,000-a-person fundraiser. The New Hampshire primary is less than a week away. She's leaving the next day to campaign there.

About fifty Washingtonians have gathered, many of them middle-aged women and many others gay men. About a third of those present are non-paying staffers there to work the crowd on Hillary's behalf. She doesn't have the time to spend on each contributor, so her 'hi ya' and 'good to see you again' will be augmented by overeducated young women from the Hillary Brigade who know what to say and how to say it. Everyone will feel Hillary's personal touch, even if only by surrogate or vicariously. All are milling in the high-ceilinged living room and hallway outside the library.

It is almost 7pm, already dark on a cold winter night. Hillary is standing in the library with her host, Max Brick, a well-known public relations firm CEO and big Democrat who owns the house. Hillary is wearing her favorite double breasted black wool jacket with matching pants, a plain white silk blouse, low-heeled black shoes. An Anne Hand designed American Flag, studded with rubies and diamonds, is pinned near her shoulder. They're talking about Brick's pending introduction of her.

She wants it right: focus on her strength as a leader, her deep concern for the middle class, for average Americans, and the fight by gays, lesbians, transgenders and women to burst through their respective lavender and glass ceilings.

Brick knows what to say, although he doesn't believe for a minute in Hillary's Concern for Regular American People, or CRAP, as he thinks of it. That is, he doesn't believe *she* believes it. Ever since Hillary Rodham shed her lower middle-class Illinois upbringing in pursuit of power, she's probably never known a working stiff she didn't want to patronize or push around. Well, "tough patootie, do your duty," as mom used to say. If you want a frigging ambassadorship, Max, you'll bust your ass to get this woman elected.

As they prepare to exit the room, a tall Secret Service agent, dark hair, dark suit and an earpiece, pushes through the door from the adjoining hallway. Moving quickly, and with determination, he pulls Brick by the arm and asks the host to cover for Hillary with the crowd.

"Something is up," he says to Brick as he leans over to Hillary and says, *sotto voce*, "We have an emergency with 'Bollocks'." 'Bollocks' is the Secret Service code name for her husband Bill, printed two weeks earlier by a columnist in the Washingtonian Magazine. The article claimed Hillary had wanted the code name for herself, since it means testicles, and she believed hers were larger than Bill's. It also claimed that Bill had convinced her to take "Timber

Wolf" instead. The Secret Service refused comment. But the article was true.

The agent tugs her arm and runs her out a side door where another agent stands, hand cupped over his ear-piece, talking out of the side of his mouth into a lapel mike. Hillary can't see his face clearly in the darkness, but that's okay. She doesn't like cops and that is what these men, and an occasional woman, are - gussied up cops.

She doesn't really know any of them anyway: she hardly ever talks with them, even though the Secret Service protective details are committed to her 24/7 as a former First Lady. She doesn't have the more elaborate 'Presidential Candidate" detail because she hasn't yet won the nomination – but, she's sure she will.

As for these security monkeys themselves, they are simply *sine qua non*, like a squad of press aides or a traveling hairdresser or a scheduler: just one more automatic perk of being an Important Person. They are dispensable and fully fungible, like the average Americans about whom she was just talking to Brick.

The two men hustle Hillary through the small garden past working caterers, out a side gate, and into a black Chevrolet war wagon parked across the sidewalk. The dim lights make it difficult to clearly ascertain what is happening, but Hillary isn't terribly worried. Although she knows virtually nothing about these men who protect her, and doesn't care, she *is* confident that they know what they are doing. She'll follow their lead until they give her an 'all clear' sign. Then she'll be back in charge.

The lead agent jumps in back with Hillary and pushes her down on the seat, whispering that she should keep still. The other agent is at the wheel already backing out onto 31st street. The lead agent throws a dark blanket over her. His hands are on her back. He can feel her trembling slightly through the blanket. She is actually not yet very afraid. She is mostly just irritated because the agent is kneading her back, probably to comfort her, but he is pushing on a long roll of fat created by her too-tight bra, similar to a kapok-stuffed canvas roll LL Bean sells to put against the bottom of a door to keep out the draft. It is humiliating for him to keep patting it.

"This is serious," he warns her. "Really serious." His tone succeeds in unsettling her. She feels a slight frisson of fear.

"More information is coming in," he says. "This has something to do with your husband. He is OK so far. But you both are in danger."

He passes a cold bottle of Fiji Water to her, telling her to drink to help calm down. She's anxious, and thirst is a natural reaction. She drinks it quickly.

Unable to see where they are going, she remains silent and under the blanket. He has finally, thank God, dropped the fat-roll squeezing.

"We just need to get to a safer place," says the agent. Her face is on his knee in the darkness. "More information is coming in but it is sketchy. Until we can get something definitive we are going to keep moving. Don't you worry your little head. We're here to protect you. I know you know that."

His deep, resonant voice is more comforting than she would have thought. And she has grown to like the warmth of his leg against her cheek.

"Don't worry your little head?" she thinks, deeply patronized. "What the fuck kind of talk is that?"

From the front seat, Hillary can hear the other agent, the driver, talking to someone. He seems to have a radio and is coordinating where they are going. He is actually talking into his closed fist. "Yes," he says, "I've got it. You have a full team there? Good. Yeah, yeah, Timber Wolf is fine. She's a trooper. Be sure you have someone ready to deliver a full brief and sit-rep to her when we arrive. OK, roger that."

As Hillary listens to the occasional chatter, they drive for five or six minutes, turning numerous times, until pulling into an open garage door in a one-lane alley behind a large house in the 3200 block of Dent Place, six blocks away.

By the time they arrive, Hillary is feeling fuzzy and drifting into semi-consciousness. Her mouth goes slack and she begins to snore, drooling warmly on the agent's knee. The phenobarbital and Ambien mixture from the Fiji Water will take a few hours to wear off. She's okay - unharmed - but she's not aware of where she is or exactly why.

The two men close the garage door and lock it from the inside with a dead bolt. The car won't leave again for a while. Neither has any clear idea of when that might be.

They carry Hillary, now with rubbery muscle control, out of the garage, across a deep, unlit backyard, passing a small pool and brick patio surrounded by many trees, and into a ground floor entrance to the back of the yellow brick house, then down stairs to the small, windowless, furnished basement – and Hillary's new home.

The basement is comfortable. A sitting room with a couch, a table, two stuffed and padded chairs, a TV, and a small refrigerator offer the first impression. Through the single door is a bedroom with a double bed made up with a cheery spread (Amish women in bonnets picking apples), a nightstand, and a small desk with a matching wood chair. A bathroom with a tub shower is attached.

The basement's only door leads up the stairs to the main level from where they just came.   It is quiet, and other than the TV, the only sounds Hillary will hear for the immediate future are those of her kidnappers - two good ol' boys from Texas.

Chapter Two

A few blocks away at Brick's house, pandemonium has broken loose. When Hillary doesn't come out to the waiting crowd in the living room, Brick goes back to look for her. She isn't there. In fact, she isn't anywhere.

Running out to a Secret Service agent in a dark blue blazer standing by the front door, Brick yells, "Where is she?"

"Where is who?" the startled agent replies.

"Mrs. Clinton, you idiot! Who else?"

The agent's stomach muscles tighten, his jaw clenches.

"Oh my frigging word," he thinks to himself. Although protocol requires an agent to be in the house in sight of Hillary at all times, she had demanded they back off - that one agent stay outside. She didn't want the sensitivities of a crowd of liberal donors, many of whom may have had horrible or even just discomforting experiences in their private lives with the police, to be annoyed by the presence of armed gorillas like these. She would not have it. She had made that clear.

Reluctantly, two of the three men in the detail have stayed outside - one at the front door, the other standing by their vehicle, surveying activity up and down N Street, fronting the house. They know the rules, but they also know that

Timber Wolf can morph into a screaming harridan in record time if her orders are defied.

They know from experience that she will pick up the phone and call the director of the Secret Service to yell about anything that pisses her off, at any time. It is easier to break the regs, take the path of least resistance, than to incur her shrieking wrath. They have broken protocol for her on many occasions before. For the first time it is going to produce particularly ugly consequences.

The agent at the car, the color of his face matching his short red hair, hears the exchange with Brick and vaults up the brick steps to the mansion to follow Brick and the other agent through the door. A panicked search through the house and backyard confirms the worst. Mrs. Clinton is gone.

Within fifteen minutes roadblocks have been set up on N Street at Wisconsin Avenue and the streets are jammed with police cars rushing to the scene: Federal Protective Police, two Park Police motorcycles with empty and pointless sidecars, D.C. police, and the Secret Service – two dozen vehicles and officers from these agencies and others. All have been routinely on post since the week following the anniversary of 9/11, from Capitol Hill and downtown through the Northwest quadrant of the city, in the event of a terrorist attack. All have arrived within minutes, including police and U.S. Coast Guard helicopters, noisy and agitated, hovering above. More police on the ground are pouring in.

All the sirens and flashing lights, on a scale unlike any ever before seen in Georgetown, immediately draw interested citizens by the hundreds from restaurants and pubs. Five TV station vans are rushing to set up on the sidewalks for live coverage.

Chapter Three

On Wisconsin Avenue, two blocks from the corner of N Street, is a tiny storefront restaurant called Tsin-Tsin (pronounced 'chin chin'). Two tables of four, four tables of two. The tiny joint, 15 feet wide and about 40 feet deep, is presided over by Mr. Wang, called "Chief" by regulars.

Tsin-Tsin is popular with some government employees from State, USAID, and DHS – particularly those who have been posted in Asia. Even a few FBI agents come in, in pairs, often once a week.

Each of the six black lacquered wood tables in Tsin-Tsin has a wireless transmitter concealed within. The small ceramic model of a U.S. Yangtze gunboat in the center of each table, which holds a single white daisy in its smoke stack, is a microphone.

A wrinkled black and white photo of Mr. Wang in a U.S. Navy chief petty officer's uniform hangs over the cash register. Mr. Wang is an excellent Cantonese cook. He speaks almost no English. His wife of 50 years has been dead for a decade.

Mrs. Wang did speak English but only Mandarin Chinese. Mr. Wang speaks only Cantonese. Regardless, years of marriage had facilitated successful nonverbal communication between them.

The Chief spent ten years cooking on the USS Penay, an American gunboat patrolling the 1,300 miles of the Yangtze River from Wuhan to Chungking. He was legendary in the Asiatic River Fleet for his Tsin-Tsin chow mein with hand made noodles. In 1941, after murderous attacks by Japanese warplanes, the U.S. river patrols ended. The boat's skipper, a Navy commander named Benton Bean, was promoted to captain. He then jumped Mr. Wang five enlisted grades, made him a Petty Officer First Class and obtained for him a U.S. entry visa.

Captain Bean moved Mr. Wang with him to his next assignment as XO of the sprawling Naval Training Center in San Diego and installed him as a cook at the Officers Club. They both retired in 1950; Mr. Wang as a Master Chief, (non-English speaking variety) and Benton Bean as a rear admiral.

Born in 1916, the Chief is 100 years old. He owns the narrow three-story wood frame building that houses Tsin-Tsin. He lives in the second floor apartment with his great granddaughter Katie, a slim, pretty woman with shoulder-length shining black hair, erect carriage, and a shapely bosom and after-deck.

Katie Wang is 30 years old but looks younger. She speaks both Mandarin and Cantonese. Her first language is English. She is a graduate of UCLA and has a Masters Degree in International Relations from George Washington University. She is both smart and beautiful.

She is Tsin-Tsin's sole waitress and cashier. She calls her great grandfather "Chief". Mr. Wang is not involved in Chinese espionage. His great granddaughter is. Katie Wang is an undercover officer with the People's Republic of China intelligence service, the Ministry of State Security, and has been seconded to the authority of the Office of the Defense Attaché at the Chinese Embassy at 3505 International Place, in Northwest Washington, less than a mile from Georgetown. Her boss is the defense attaché himself, Major General Xu Donfang.

The Chief, in his white Haynes T-shirt, canvas pants and soiled apron, trots from the restaurant behind a handful of dinner patrons, all flowing with the crowd to the corner of N Street, drawn by the flashing police lights, sirens and general din of the choppers above. Katie follows in their wake in tight black pants and low heels.

In downtown Washington, a mile away on 15th Street, the evening shift of a dozen reporters and editors at the Washington Post newsroom has gathered around a ceiling TV over the City Desk. The story is being practically shouted to the audience by excited cable news anchors, all competing feverishly for the story of the year, maybe even the decade, like starving rats finding a fresh pack of Ding Dongs.

Chapter Four

To the north, in New York City, Arthur Ochs Sulzberger, Junior, publisher of the New York Times, known popularly, but only behind his back, as "Pinch" (in contrast to his popular father, "Punch," now departed, whom he succeeded), is in the front passenger seat of a limousine, in traffic, at the corner of 72nd Street and Park Avenue in Manhattan. Pinch plans to exit soon and likes to appear humble when he alights in front of a crowd, which is why he is not in the back.

Pinch is on his way to a black-tie dinner for the Environmental Defense Fund. He looks dapper as always, but as he told his latest wife, Gabrielle Greene, the tough California venture capitalist, when she called him today after a Whole Foods Board of Director's meeting, he has a genuinely negative interest in the EDF event. He's going, as he told her, because he has been pressured to attend by a boorish cousin who is on the Times board and to whom he is obliged to be nice.

He's close to being there when his cell phone rings. He casually picks it up and looks to see who is calling.

"Oh Christ," he thinks. It's his wife, Gail. She is really his ex-wife, Gail. Gail Gregg. They have been divorced for five years and he has a new wife, a fact that sometimes slips his mind. Pinch, now 64, was married to Gail for 33 years, with occasional time off for separations - he gets

24

mixed up about this, too, often feeling they are still together.

"Ever notice, Arthur, that both of your wives have the initials GG? Do you think that means anything?" said his friend from boarding school, Prosser Melton, the other day at lunch at The Russian Tea Room.

"I've never thought of it," said Pinch, holding his $45 lobster roll firmly, like it might escape and head back to Kennebunkport. He could tell by the spark in Prosser's slightly crossed eyes that this was leading up to one of his lame jokes.

"OK, Pross, I'll bite. Go."

"Well, the thought occurred, when I noticed four "G's" in two names, that my friend Arthur has been on a subconscious quest for the ultimate 'G spot.' Am I right?"

"What's a 'G spot'?" asked Arthur, the lobster roll close to his lips, thereby giving Prosser a much better punch line when he retold the story later for the amusement of mutual friends.

"Gail," thinks Pinch. The pair had separated years ago, when she learned, or at least came to believe, that he was banging Caroline Kennedy and had hung horns on Gail's head, and also on the head of that pitiful and weird Edward Schlossberg, Caroline's long suffering husband. Whatever did happen between him and Caroline, only the

25

two of them know for sure, and they had agreed to never tell anyone, certainly not Gail. They had stuck to their promise.

Caroline was no intellectual - quite the opposite. She had been a total disaster as a candidate to replace Hillary when Hillary left her Senate seat for the State Department honcho's job. Caroline floundered so horribly at a news conference that the blind Governor Dave Patterson, who had planned to appoint her to the vacant Senate seat changed his back-stabbing mind after the media began counting the number of times Caroline mumbled "um" and "you know" and "like." More than a hundred times, it turned out. Total frigging disaster. She withdrew her name, much to Patterson's relief.

It wasn't over for her though. Obama gave her the ambassador's job in Tokyo, where she could say "um" and "you know" and add "like" to every descriptive sentence she uttered to all those little people and they'd believe she is speaking a pidgin Japanese. Thinking about it, Pinch chortles to himself.

"Oh, Jeez, what does Gail want?" he thinks. "This is never good."

He answers.

"Hillary has been snatched!" his former wife blurts excitedly. "Kidnapped in Washington, D.C.!"

26

"Oh, my God," Pinch replies. Gail is crying. She was always stronger than Pinch, unbending, decisive, nobody to fuck with. She never cries.

Hearing her tears, Pinch begins to cry too. He loves Hillary, he loves that she is so tough. He intends to throw the whole weight of the Times behind Hillary if she captures New Hampshire, even though the Times' political heft, and its profitability, have dwindled considerably under Pinch's leadership.

Another call is beeping. He gets rid of Gail, relieved that she isn't trying to squeeze him for any more dough.

It is the elderly News Queen, as he is known, Bruce Gelb from the National Lesbian and Gay Journalists Association. Bruce works for the Times and is an ardent Hillary supporter, as are most of the NLGJA members, who number more than a hundred at the Times.

Pinch wipes a tear off his cheek. "Arthur, did you hear?" Bruce says, his voice cracking.

Pinch begins to cry all over again, and Brucie joins him.

"I'm going to the newsroom tonight," says Pinch. "We'll form a journalistic task force. We will find out what happened and who did it and why. The old Gray Lady will find Hillary."

Pinch sounds convincing, but he isn't really. He doesn't know enough yet about what happened to be convinced of anything.

"We will see that the fascist, anti-democratic forces that took her will be punished, their scrawny necks rung until they are dead," he blurts out hopefully.

Chapter Five

Two months earlier two white men in their mid-60's are seated in a duck blind in a riverine marsh near Frisco, Texas. It's a chilly early morning and the sun is rising over the horizon. The ducks are no longer flying. Their two dogs, wearing cammo vests, are sitting next to a small pile of dead birds outside the blind.

The men are hunkered on a wet bench ruminating about the pathetic economic conditions and the general decline of America. They've been out since 4am, plenty of time for lots of chatter. Now the subject is the rapid social and cultural disintegration of the United States. The men are third-generation Texans and are deeply patriotic.

"The country is racing downhill and we are going to get Hillary Clinton as our next President," says one of them, a man named Earl.

"She's worse than that twat-hound of a husband," says the other. His name is Bobby.

"The New Hampshire primary is coming up and if she takes it she'll have a lock on the convention in August."

"Hell," says Earl. "She probably already does. She'll be our next President at this rate. We are so screwed."

Both of them fidget, wincing at the nightmare notion.

"I got an idea," says Earl Hines, who has just sold his HVAC company for $11 million, making him the senior of the two men - at least in his own eyes.

Earl was nicknamed "Fatha" fifty years earlier, after a black musician of the same name - Earl "Fatha" Hines from Chicago, famous in the jazz world in years gone by. The African-American Earl Hines was older than many of his musician friends. Fatha meant "father."

Earl thinks the original Fatha played piano but he isn't sure of that and he, himself, doesn't give a fuck about music anyway. His boyhood friends loved pretending Earl was a Negro, which is why they gave him the nickname, thinking it annoyed him. But it didn't.

Earl is the father of three girls, now grown. He has been married to the same woman for forty years. They have six grandchildren. Earl, like his namesake, is a little overweight.

"Let's grab her, shrink-wrap the bitch, and tuck her away until after the New Hampshire primary vote. We won't hurt her. And if we do it right, we won't get caught. We will have performed a genuine patriotic duty. We can probably never tell our grandchildren, but *we'll* know." Hines revels in the thought.

He doesn't explain why grabbing her is going to forestall her winning the primary, but it doesn't matter. It has the sound of an excellent idea.

Bobby Crandall, slight and balding, has retired from his small general insurance agency after 46 years. He likes the idea immediately, and then admires it even more when Fatha says, "I'll put up the dough. We can probably do it for fifty grand or less. I'll find a way to write it off."

"Now you're talking," says Crandall, warming to the excitement of it all.

"Shrink-wrap her. Wow," he exclaims. "I wish I could do that to Louella. At least to cover her mouth. The woman can yammer for an hour at a time, nonstop."

Totally psyched by the conversation, Crandall rubs his chin and looks away from the now-rising sun. "Good thing for those birds that none of them are flying by right now," he thinks to himself. "I'd knock them right out of the sky!"

The idea of kidnapping a possible future president and getting a tax deduction for the expenses tickles the bejesus out of both men. They chortle and cackle as they share an early morning beer sitting on the wet bench of the reed-covered blind, warming by the rising sun and talking about how best to get it done. This is the way those Texas country boys do things. A few ducks, a few beers, some palaver. A few ducks, a few beers, more chatter. But the ducks are all done flying this morning, so for now it's just drinking beer and more talking.

Crandall shuffles on the bench and says, "Do you know Wayne Wayne over at the Wal-Mart? Wayne B. Wayne. Funny name. He runs the anti-shoplifting squad. Merchandise control officers, they call 'em. He's smart, but he knows his place. He could use some dough. His wife, Rae Anne, left him and she took the kids, his truck and the dog, too. Sad. He's a tough boy. He was a constable over at the Hyde Township for a few years. He knows about security and stuff like that. Lets talk to him tomorrow."

Out of beer, the two men part ways and head home. The following day they meet at the local McDonalds.

Chapter Six

Cable and network television is suddenly alive with activity. American Idol is interrupted for a flash news bulletin. On MSNBC, Rachel Maddow is on the air live.

She has half risen from her anchor chair as a lightweight pundit named Melissa Harris-Perry runs into the studio, interrupting a live interview by Rachel with Gloria Steinem. Harris-Perry is shouting. She appears deranged.

Steinem, soon to be 82 years old, has been telling Maddow about growing up in a trailer park in Toledo, Ohio, and landing at Smith College in Northampton, Massachusetts, where she developed homicidal feminist chops. It's a story she's told for almost sixty years but the media never tires of it and she revels in the attention.

"You changed America," Maddow has just said, her eyes shining. "You freed millions of American women from the testosterone-fed chains that bound them." Steinem is glowing with pride.

Harris-Perry is waving a wire service bulletin and yelling unintelligibly. Maddow leaps up, confused, as the Harris-Perry woman shouts, "Oh my God, Rachel. Holy fuck. Oh, fuck me. Hillary has been kidnapped." The microphones pick up every word.

Maddow stands in disbelief, her mouth agape, lost in the moment.

Steinem, who is wearing 1960's style tinted aviator glasses and has left her aluminum walker hidden behind the desk, slumps in her seat, like a vacuum cleaner bag from which the air has just been sucked.

Maddow grabs the bulletin. She is thinking that Harris-Perry, whom she doesn't really like that much, will be in deep shit with the NBC suits about dropping multiple "F" words on live air. Maddow's voice is calm but wavers slightly.

"This just in," she says, her words oozing portent as she looks directly into the camera. She has never actually been a news anchor, always a liberal pundit, but the thought of sounding like Walter Cronkite moistens her loins.

"Hillary Clinton appears to have been kidnapped from a home in Georgetown. This happened minutes ago. Two suspects, apparently posing as Secret Service Agents, grabbed her and were seen bundling her into a black SUV and racing away."

The bulletin itself is just a couple of sentences. Maddow skillfully ad libs what has not yet been written:

"The New Hampshire Primary is just a week away. Secretary Clinton, former First lady, former Senator from New York, a symbol of strength and courage to women around the world, is the front-runner. This is a global tragedy in the making."

She pauses for effect, as if to gather her thoughts.

"A plot by rightwing extremists is suspected in this incredibly obscene crime, though we have no definitive word as yet as to who is responsible." The 'right-wing extremists' is ad-libbing at its best since no one really knows anything at all about who has done this, but Maddow throws it out authoritatively.

"I am going to break for a commercial. We will collect ourselves and seek more information for you. Again, Hillary Clinton has been kidnapped. Don't go away."

Gloria Steinem, who has been running her stubby, arthritic fingers through her hair, looks increasingly frazzled.

Harris-Perry is crying. Maddow puts her arm around her in a fatherly manner as the other woman sobs, and the director, as stunned as anyone, cuts to a commercial.

An ad for "Align," a pro-biotic, appears and an attractive woman begins talking about her problems with constipation. Harris-Perry says, to no one in particular, her lips quivering, "The right wing did this?" The studio microphones are hot and the audience hears this exchange over the tale of "gas and bloating" from the TV ad.

"I don't actually know that, at least not yet," says Maddow, clenching a fist. "But I'd fucking bet on it. Probably Tea Baggers or those frigging Romney Mormons."

Maddow will herself soon be joining Harris-Perry, treading barefoot in seriously deep shit when NBC executives listen to the tape of what she has said and the complaints begin to pour in.

"Hillary Clinton has been kidnapped!" travels at the speed of lightening from thousands of lips to millions of incredulous ears and soon reverberates around the world.

Chapter Seven

Fatha Hines and Bobby Crandall are seated already when Wayne B. Wayne and Billy Fly come in. Crandall introduces the two of them to Fatha, and small talk takes place over coffee and four Happy Meals.

Fatha isn't quite ready to jump into this venture until he believes his money will be well spent and the chances of getting caught appear exceedingly low. He looks at the two of them carefully, liking what he sees and hears.

Wayne is the bigger of the two, and he presents himself well.

"Yes," he says when asked, he knows about security, and he even worked some undercover jobs when he was a constable. "You know, drug deals and stuff like that. I know how to do them," he says. "I can be a pretty crafty fella when need be."

"I did a little private eye work a few years back," he says. "A fella I knew, his wife worked in the County Supervisor's Office over in Raymond. He suspected she was cheating on him. He wanted me to find out. I put her under surveillance for a week and, whaddaya know, three days into it I find out she is banging one of the supervisors. Man named Gonzales. Fat guy; everybody called him "Speedy," cause he was so not. She was a tad homely, I have to say, a face like a busted fence. But that puss was on a world class body, and she smelled good, a beautiful ass and a pair of boobs that looked like they had a life of their own."

"Well, what did the husband say when you told him?" Fatha asks.

"Ha, Jeez, I *never* told the boy. I braced her in the motel parking lot, a joint called the Do Drop, off highway 83. Speedy was still inside sleeping off their tumble. I told her I knew she had been cheating and that her hubby had hired me. She looked me over and said, how about us making this a barter deal? You don't rat me out and I will trade you something you'll like, big time. I'm not talking about money."

"I hopped in her car and we drove around back. She pulled out those amazing boobs and we went at it like teenyboppers. We shook hands before she left. I called her husband at the end of the week and said she was as innocent as Snow White 'fore she met the Dwarfs."

Fatha Hines chuckles and dips a French fry into a pool of catsup he has squeezed on his Big Mac wrapper. He pops it between his lips and says, "Good story, Wayne. I like an enterprising self-starter and you obviously are one."

He turns to Wayne's friend Billy Fly. Fly is called Zipper by all his buddies. He is only working part-time at Walmart but is quiet and looks presentable.

"How about you, boy," says Fatha, looking at Zipper. "If you're going to work for me you need to sit up straight. Quit slouching. You need to have good posture in this new position. Show a little pride, boy, because if I hire you, you will be going to Washington, D.C., on an important assignment. All expenses paid," he adds.

Actually, Zipper already possesses a small reservoir of genuine pride, via a personal and unusual talent, though few of the local older folks are aware of it.

Billy was well known among his Frisco High School friends for his remarkable ability to urinate over a 1949 Ford convertible, a car that he owned and kept in perfect condition. Zipper could stand by the driver's door, huff and puff and tighten his face muscles in theatrical concentration, and send a steady stream of water across to the other side with nary a drop hitting the car. He had performed this feat on demand for dozens of boys and a few girls.

Someone once proposed they write the International Olympic Committee and see if it could become a legitimate competition. Zipper was flattered but did wonder how they would ever get that on TV. Regardless he never heard any more about it.

Fatha likes these guys. It's easy. No phony moves required here. Two good old boys picking two other good old boys for something no one has ever tried before - the kidnapping of a Presidential candidate.

To Fatha, and to Bobby by default, these fellas are an excellent fit for the job. They have the needed chutzpah for this to work. "Chutzpah" means brass balls in the Jewish language, someone once told him, though he has not a clue as to how to spell it. Not needed anyway because none of this is going to be written down.

"I want you guys to get cleaned up a bit and be back here Friday morning," Fatha says. "Here's some money. Get haircuts. Get real 'sidewalls.' Look sharp. We'll sit down again and talk about what me and Crandall here want you to do. You are going to be traveling, boys."

Chapter Eight

By midnight, just hours after Hillary's disappearance, the city of Washington, D.C., is buzzing almost loud enough to be heard in Virginia and Maryland. It's as if a swarm of 17-year-cycle cicadas is hiding in every tree and under every bush.

The Secretary of Homeland Security and the Director of the Secret Service are holding a joint news conference that is so crowded they have to move it from the Secretary's conference room into Homeland's main auditorium.

There's no lack of participation. Dozens of Obama administration appointees and federal law enforcement agency employees are joined by dozens of news crews and more than a hundred reporters and TV correspondents. More are on their way from around the globe, but they won't make it tonight. Crowds of the curious have even assembled on the streets nearby, bracing against the cold in hopes of learning something from those leaving the news conference.

Homeland Security has moved into the former site of St. Elizabeth's Hospital for the Insane in Anacostia, across the river in southeast Washington, D.C. St. Elizabeth's was active as a federal loony bin for a hundred years; the poet Ezra Pound spent a dozen years here, locked up for treason after WWII. He had made radio broadcasts in support of Mussolini, whom he admired.

Homeland Security, bivouacked with more than 1,000 federal mental patients, is now the butt of many jokes. TV reporters feeling nasty will sometimes sign off as "coming to you live from the U.S. Government's Rubber Room." No humor tonight, though. The air itself seems deadly serious.

The Secretary and the Director sit at a table flanked on both sides and behind by Deputy Director of the FBI, Denny Walsh; the D.C. Chief of Police, Cathy Lanier, a former welfare mother very popular with the media; Tawanna Brown, Chief of the U.S. Park Police; Shirley Dogatz, Chief of the Secret Service Uniformed Division; Winifred Wittlesley, Director of U.S. Customs and Border Security (the old U.S. Border Patrol); Admiral Bonnie Gintling, Commandant of the U.S. Coast Guard; Polly Barton, the new chief of the Federal Protective Service; Mary Swizzler, Chief of the Capitol Hill Police; Jennifer Lanniston, Director of the ATF; and delegate Eleanor Holmes Norton, the non-voting member of Congress from the District of Columbia and a notorious publicity hound.

Holmes-Norton, 79, wearing a short and curly reddish-blonde wig, wasn't invited. She is not about to miss any promotional political opportunities and has pushed her way in. No one challenges her. It isn't worth the effort. She is shrill and aggressive. They all know that if she is barred from the news conference she'd be on the local news in the morning lobbing racism and sexism anti-personnel grenades.

Holmes Norton had "forgotten" to file federal income tax returns for eight straight years, and had, when charged, shifted all the blame onto her now late husband, Ed Norton, Chairman of the Washington, D.C., Board of Elections & Ethics. He was widely known as the Black Caspar Milquetoast and also called "No Nads Norton".

All of this had happened on the eve of Eleanor's first congressional election. The Washington Post called on her to quit and deemed her "unqualified".

She made Ed hold a news conference on the sidewalk in front of her campaign headquarters, at which he said, "I am the villain. Blame me. I just kept putting off filing." (Ed and Eleanor, both lawyers, had put off filing or paying for the years 1982 through 1989.) Holmes Norton won the election against her principal opponent, a white woman, anyway a few days later.

The body weight on the stage is so heavy, and so concentrated in a small area that a D.C. fire marshal warns that it could collapse, on live TV yet. She's ignored, and the news conference marches on.

The Secret Service Director admits that it appears the kidnappers were posing as his agents. There were, he says, three actual agents at the party - one inside the party itself, one sitting outside in front on N Street in a parked war wagon, and the other in a follow car. All were following basic protocol and there were no known specific threats against Mrs. Clinton. The one agent inside had seen the kidnappers but thought they were guests as they mingled with the crowd. He is now working with artists to create composite drawings of the two suspects.

Over continual reportorial shouting of questions from the frenzied media mob, the Director says that Mrs. Clinton had demanded of her supervisory agent that he let her meet with the host, Mr. Maxwell Brick, alone for ten minutes in the library, and he had acceded to her wishes.

Yes, the Director has ordered a complete investigation and that has already begun. (It hasn't, since the agents involved have already hired Joe DiGenova and Victoria Toensing, a couple of married kick-ass former prosecutors who specialize in tormenting the government when it misbehaves with their clients.) The only thing the Director will say at this time, in defense of the Service, is that the one agent inside didn't see the fake agents go through the library doors because there were so many people blocking his view and he was distracted for a moment. What the Director doesn't know is that the agent was actually chatting up a perky new Hillary campaign staffer wearing an almost sheer blouse without a bra.

The two men who grabbed Hillary and bundled her into a black SUV were imposters, he says, as if it were not now

44

obvious. We have a photo of one of the men, said the Director, taken by a waiter who was near the car when he spotted Mrs. Clinton and wanted her picture to show friends. This was just when she was shuffled into the back seat, which the waiter, upon reflection, thought was odd.

The Secret Service Director doesn't show the photo and refuses to give copies, though there is a loud demand from reporters. The Director has just seen it himself. It is blurry and only shows part of the fake agent's face and nothing of the SUV's license plate. The picture is being analyzed, he says, though there is no analysis left to perform.

He does say that witnesses identified both of the men as clean-cut, tall and white, in their early 30's. They are working with witnesses on the specific descriptions of each man.

The Washington Post soon gets its own copy of the picture and runs it on the front page. On the first day it sparks more than 1000 calls from people who want to help, have possible information (often about suspicious neighbors or deranged ex-boyfriends), or who think they have seen Hillary or the kidnappers.

Some have spotted the suspects on the Metro, others in a 7/Eleven buying Big Gulps or sharing a supersize bag of Dorritos; a woman from Compton, California, a depressing suburb of LA, swears she had been on a Southwest Air flight the day before from Monterrey,

Mexico, with the two kidnappers, who sat together across the aisle and glowered at her and other passengers.

Another woman believes the pair had been on her flight from Phoenix to Reagan National Airport in Washington, dressed identically in pink golf shirts, green Madras Bermuda shorts, white tube sox and black leather laced shoes. They had been loudly chewing gum, and, unlike the police artist's renderings, they sported heavily waxed crew cuts with matching peroxide blonde streaks in front.

"Ma'am," says the Task Force operator, "that just doesn't fit the description at all."

"I know," says the caller. "I'm not stupid. But I could see it was them, *underneath!* They were wearing *disguises*."

Law enforcement's work has just begun and much of it is reminiscent to reporters and police alike of the D.C. sniper case in 2002, wherein thousands of leads from well intentioned citizens led absolutely nowhere but consumed many thousands of man hours.

By the end of the D.C. sniper case, ten people had been killed and three others severely wounded. John Muhammad, 41, and Lee Malvo, 17, homosexual lovers and Islamic religious fanatics, were tried and convicted. At the trial they testified that they wanted to start a "jihad" and bring America to its knees. John Allen Muhammad was executed by lethal injection in 2009 at Virginia's

46

Greenville Correctional Facility in Jarratt, Virginia. His teenage lover, Lee Boyd Malvo, is now serving six consecutive life sentences at the maximum security Red Onion State Prison in Pound, Virginia.

Every guest and every neighbor on both sides of N Street for four blocks will be interrogated, says Homeland Security Secretary Jeh Johnson.

"Just call me 'Jay'," he tells reporters, alluding to the odd spelling of his first name.

He has said this before, when he was flacking as a lawyer for the Pentagon and explaining that President Obama had every right to summarily execute by unmanned drone a U.S. citizen, an Islamist, and his son in Yemen, because he and Obama (a friend of Jeh's) had designated them as terrorists.

Johnson had upset many people by telling the U.S. Conference of Mayors, a month after he was sworn in at DHS and given practical control of the country's borders, that more that 11 million illegal aliens "who are already in the country, have earned the right to be citizens."

"We have some leads," Johnson says, "but we can't talk about them."

They can't talk about them because he is lying. They don't actually have any leads - not one. But, by implying they might be on the trail of the perps could unsettle the kidnappers and pressure them into making a discoverable mistake.

"We are applying old-fashioned shoe-leather detective work, pounding pavements and squeezing likely informants. More than two hundred detectives and criminal investigators, from agencies as diverse as the U.S. Postal Service to the Capitol Park Police, have been assigned to work under the FBI at the Find Hillary Task Force, the FHTF, to be headquartered in downtown Washington so it will be more easily accessible to all agencies and the White House."

In fact, thinks Jeh Johnson, we have been praying for the emergence of a credible snitch but not one has slid out from under a frigging rock —and one never will.

The caterers say Mrs. Clinton appeared to be leaving voluntarily with the fake agents. No weapons were seen. No cries or appeals for help. No shots fired. A black SUV, such as the Secret Service uses, was seen by caterers in the driveway at the back and side of the house, pulling away just after Hillary was observed moving swiftly through the garden.

Security cameras throughout the neighborhood are being reviewed for any applicable information. No ransom or kidnap demands have been received. No one has claimed responsibility. The weight of the full Federal government is behind finding her and bringing her home safely. Her own Secret Service detail clearly made a mistake and yes, there will be a full investigation into what happened.

"Is it true that Mrs. Clinton's code-name with the Secret Service is 'Honey Badger'," yells a frizzy-haired woman reporter from Reuters?

"We don't comment on classified designators," says Johnson. In fact, Hillary's "*nom de geurre*" is Timber Wolf, thinks Johnson, who has hung onto his high school French. She had previously been called Major Tom but she didn't like it, the Secret Service has told him, because Bill made fun of it. ("Calling Major Tom") She is fond of the name Timber Wolf, and sometimes growls playfully at her detail members but only when she is in a good mood, which isn't often, they have said.

The Secretary introduces FBI deputy director Dennis Walsh, head of the Bureau's Criminal Investigative Division, who will lead the task force in the investigation.

"We will find Mrs. Clinton. We will bring her home," Walsh says, as he bends over a table mike, his massive bulk pushing Delegate Norton to the side.

Walsh then refuses to answer any questions, including one shouted by Richard Cohen of the Washington Post, who looks agitated, and yells, "Bring her home *alive*, did you mean to say, Mr. Walsh?"

Walsh glares and doesn't respond. He has always thought the white bearded Cohen, with a face as red as a boiled tomato, is an unregenerate liberal assbite, like most of his WaPo colleagues.

The rest of the news conference plods on.

"Only one thing can be counted on for certain," TV anchor Megyn Kelly says on Fox, broadcasting her show the Kelly File live from the former Rubber Room at St Elizabeth's Hospital. "Hillary Clinton is gone, and no one knows where she is."

A few feet behind Kelly, standing on the concourse outside the mammoth DHS building, viewers can see mop-haired Reagan assassin John Hinckley, newly furloughed by a Federal Judge from St Elizabeth's for week-long sleepovers with his mother in Virginia – allowed to drive there alone in his new car, waving shyly with his fingers to the camera (and maybe even to Jody Foster.)

Hinckley is often seen wandering around DHS where they consider him goofy and harmless. Of course they thought that in 2014 when after years of an agonized life former press secretary Jim Brady finally died from the head wounds given to him by Hinckley.

Next to Hinckley in the camera shot is another man, who would not be recognized by the viewers that day. He is also a patient at St. E's and a friend of Hinckley's, a shoe salesman from Annapolis, Maryland, named Lothar Menzel, a sometimes incredibly violent schizophrenic who regularly escapes from St. E's, often just jogging through a gate as a car enters or exits. He is easily identifiable as he is missing both thumbs, having chewed them off and eaten them. He has been locked up since 1998 for various crimes, his last in 2010 for trying to murder a hospital orderly. An outfit called the D.C. Department of Behavioral Health oversees St. E's. Like most D.C. government institutions, the DBH has a reputation for pathetic sloth and inefficiency.

.

Chapter Nine

Hillary wakes in a small, warm room without windows. Light comes from an inexpensive chandelier hanging from the ceiling. She's on a double bed with a pillow and what look like clean sheets, blanket and a spread.

Her head aches. She feels like shit and she is sure that she looks it, too. Even her teeth hurt. Her tongue feels like it has been wrapped in lint from a clothes dryer. Her stomach is rumbling. She's slightly nauseous and hungry at the same time.

She is also still confused. She thinks about the Fiji water and realizes she was drugged. She is scared, but more than that she is angry and quickly becoming furious. "Where am I? Who were those Secret Service men? Where is Bill? Where is Huma? What the hell is going on?"

Soon she is fit to be frigging tied. She looks around the room. It's bare except for the bed she's sitting on, two chairs, a small desk, and the light overhead. The paint is old and yellow. The floor is concrete but covered with a faded oriental rug. There is no window and no closet - just one door in the wall opposite the bed and a small connecting bathroom with sink, toilet and tub. She is gaining her strength back. She starts yelling.

One of the faux-agents opens the door and comes in the room. She hasn't really looked at him before and she doesn't recognize him now. Actually, she would barely recognize any of the agents who work for her. The only one she does know is the lead agent of her overall detail, Duane Terry. She knows him because he is responsible for all of the minion agents who work with her on a daily basis. Terry briefs her on occasion and she vents to him about the "goons" she has to put up with. But she secretly loves the fact that she has a security detail, the envy of all of Washington without them.

"Where am I?" she barks. She's standing, wobbling a bit. "Tell me where the hell I am! What the fuck is going on here? Where are my people? Who are you?"

The agent looks at her for a moment, taken aback by her coarse language. It's standard palaver for her away from the public ear and well known to hundreds of staffers who worked for her for the past twenty years and equally well known to Bill who has been the frequent target of her creatively profane ire.

"Listen you asshole," she continues. "I want out of here right now. What is going on? I want to hear it from someone higher in the chain than you. Where's my husband? What has happened to him?"

The door opens slightly, enough for someone to look in, and then the other agent opens it fully and enters. He's bigger than the first agent. Hillary starts towards the door, shoving the smaller agent aside and is about to try the same with the second man when she stumbles and loses her footing. The big agent catches her arm and steadies her.

"Out of the frigging way, buster," she yells. The second agent stands in her path directly at the door and plants his feet firmly on the floor. He's big – maybe a little taller than his partner - about six feet two but fuller and more muscular, probably 200 pounds. He looks determined.

"You're not leaving this room, Mrs. Clinton. You are safer here. We have orders," he says. The phony agent looks down at her in a resolute manner, but she is undeterred.

She gets up under his nose and states firmly, "I want to talk to Agent Terry right now! Your boss! And I know the Secretary of the Treasury, your big boss. And I know the head of Homeland Security. This is such incredible bullshit. I demand to know what's going on!"

The big one says, "Ma'am, we work for the Secret Service. We are part of the Presidential Protection Unit. We don't work for the Treasury Secretary or the Homeland Security person, either. No way. Our outfit is the Secret Service."

He's lying. It's obvious. He's not even good at it. What a loser. She has told a lot of lies in her life but not one was as lamely delivered as this guy's. Pathetic. Besides, she notices, his suit is cheap and he has missed some stubble on his chin. No agent is ever unkempt.

"Who *are* you, ass wipe?" she demands. "Just who the hell are you?"

"Well, we sure aren't no 'treasurians' or 'homelanders' either," says the smaller agent.

In an instant, Hillary is steaming mad - out of control. She looks at the bigger of the two and says, "Do you know who you are fucking with here? I killed Vince Foster and I'll kill you, you mammy-jammer. I will murder your wife and kids and your damned three-legged dog. You let me out of here right now, you stupid schmuck."

The two men are taken aback, intimidated by her vitriolic tone and by the intensity of her language.

"Ah, ma'am we haven't been swearing at you, out of respect, so please don't be swearing at us. We don't like it and it is unbecoming to you as an important person and as a woman."

"Respect? You frigging moron," she says. "You kidnapped me, scared the shit out of me, probably for the rest of my life, and *you don't want to disrespect me*? Get a life. And what do you mean, 'as a woman'. Women have just as much right to swear as men. Women's rights are human rights. Remember that. Now unlock that door and get out of the way, bud."

Neither of them moves.

"We can't do that," says the bigger one. "We are holding you for your own safety, ma'am. We have to keep you here for a little bit longer until everyone is safe. We'll bring some breakfast down soon. It's from Roy Rogers. It's got biscuits and honey and them little fried potatoes. It's real good."

"Roy Rogers? Are you fucking kidding me? Is Dale Evans going to serve it? I'm not eating crap like that, you scum-sucking idiot."

"Mrs. Clinton," Wayne B. Wayne says, exasperated. "I'm One. That's my name to you. Call me that, please. My friend there is Two."

"You call him 'Two'?" she says, looking at Zipper with narrowed eyes of contempt. "He doesn't look Vietnamese to me."

The men stand in silent confusion. She pauses. "That's a joke, stupid," she says calmly. "I don't care what your names are. You'll both be swinging from a federal yardarm by the time I'm through with you. Screw you both."

She actually doesn't know what a yardarm is. She likes the gallows-y sound of it. She has always meant to look it up on Google but never has.

"Did you really kill Vince Foster?" the smaller one asks.

"Of course I didn't kill him," she says through clenched teeth. "He was my boyfriend. He killed *himself.* Probably because I would never leave my husband for him, if you care. But that doesn't mean I'm not going to kill you, you vapid motherfucker. And you can stick those biscuits up your ass while you are at it."

Zipper recoils at her venom and she takes a swing at him. She misses, but the bump in his otherwise straight nose gives testimony to the fact that he's probably been in a few bar fights. Hitting him probably wouldn't have mattered much. She aims a short kick at his crotch. Zipper catches her foot before it connects and holds her by the ankle, almost tipping her over backward.

Wayne B. Wayne, now called One, appears to be in charge. He grabs her from behind and restrains her arms. He's not overly forceful, but she clearly can't get away.

"Sorry, Ma'am," he says. "I don't want you to hurt yourself or either one of us. We're not here to let anyone get hurt."

Wayne shuffles her over towards one of the wooden chairs and his partner tells her to sit while he handcuffs her to the leg of the desk. She calms down, looking around the room for anything she can use as a weapon. She realizes she can lift the desk and slide the handcuff link off the leg bottom, but there's nothing to be gained from it right now. These guys are too big. She'll bide her time.

"What are you going to do to me?" she asks curtly. "What exactly is this all about?"

"Ma'am, we're going to let you go when this is over. Right now we just need you to do what we tell you to do. And at this very moment that means settle down. Like I said, we're not going to hurt you and we don't want you to hurt us."

"Ah, screw you both. Annoying jerks," she mumbles under her breath.

"I want to let my husband know I'm okay," she says suddenly. "It's important. He's probably worried to death. He has a heart condition. He's not well. Where's my phone? Do you have my phone?"

"I've got it here," Wayne responds. He pulls it out of his pocket. He'd taken it from her when she was lying in the back seat of the sedan, sedated and unaware of what was going on. The moment he grabbed it he turned it off and yanked the SIM card, so that no cell signals would be picked up, giving away their general location.

"I want to send Bill a text message," she says. "I want to do it now."

"Okay, Mrs. Clinton. We'll do it for you. I don't see any harm in that. We don't want him to have a heart attack."

Wayne has always liked Bill Clinton. He has heard about all those women Clinton screwed and he both approves and is envious.

Zipper gets curious and looks in her small handbag. He notices a container of pills and pulls it out. The label reads "Beano."

Wayne says to Hillary, "What are these for?" having no real clue. Her face reddens slightly. Her attacks of unexpected kamikaze flatulence, as Bill calls them, are well known to those closest to her though hardly a topic of conversation.

She remembers the first time it had happened in front of others. It was in New Haven, during the vigil she and Bill had joined outside the Bobby Seale Black Panther Party murder trial. She and Bill were sleeping on somebody's floor under a heavy Hudson Bay blanket. The unexpected eruption was so loud it woke them both, and perhaps even others in the room (they were all working to save Bobby Seale from outrageous prosecutorial harassment).

Bill, such a pig at times, seemed to be the first to know what woke them. To her mortification, he yelled, "Dutch Oven," and began flapping the blanket like Tonto sending smoke signals. Forty years of sometimes sleeping in the same bed hasn't diminished the humiliating memory for Hillary.

"None of your frigging business," she says to Zipper, who is holding the Beano bottle. "It is a kind of medicine, for indigestion. It is made from garbanzo beans. Stop asking me all these questions." Wayne drops the pills back in her purse.

Wayne holds the phone up and turns it on. Without the SIM card, which he had removed earlier, the phone can't be tracked or identified. It's good for music, games, pictures, time, and many other applications. But without the SIM card it's not good for communications.

"What name is your husband on your contact list?" Wayne asks. "What do you want to say?"

"It's under 'Slick'," she responds.

"Slick?" Wayne thinks. Wayne remembers the negative nickname, "Slick Willy," but he doesn't ask if that's the reference. He pulls Slick up on the contacts list and presses the icon for text message. The text screen pops up, ready for the message.

Hillary dictates it: "Bill, I'm OK. They say they will let me go. Hillary."

Wayne says, "Don't you want to add 'love' to this? Like 'Love, Hillary'?"

"Oh, yeah. Fine - go ahead," she replies.

The message is ready. Wayne drops the i-phone into his pocket. It'll be a few days before the telephone is turned back on, the SIM card inserted, and the 'send' button hit.

They lock Hillary in the room.

"She's plenty tough. She almost nailed me with that kick, says Zipper. "She's got some big legs on her. She could kick start an 18-wheeler, no doubt."

Chapter Ten

Law enforcement authorities on every level and of every possible description have been thrown into an almost immediate delirious fugue. From the FBI's central Headquarters in the sprawling J. E. Hoover building on Pennsylvania Avenue in Washington, D.C., down to auxiliary police officers in every little hamlet and village, at first along the East Coast from Maine to Florida, but within 24 hours to include the entire country, all have been contacted by Homeland Security and received fliers with a description of Hillary Clinton, a précis of the crime, and a description and composite drawing of the two kidnappers. Millions are distributed.

Two fliers are tacked to the Frisco, Texas, post office bulletin board when Billy Crandall stops by to pick up some mail the next morning. "Well, my word," he says to himself. "Lookee, lookee here."

There are too many people moving in and out of the lobby to pull one of the sheets down to bring to show Fatha. He will just send him over to see it himself. He is pleased to note that neither drawing looks anything like Zipper or Wayne.

Within a few more hours, 140,000 armed and sworn police officers (those entitled to make an arrest) and another 100,000 part time officers (including 50,000 who are also sworn and carry at least one gun) employed by 18,000 state and local law enforcement agencies across the country, from outfits as different as Alcohol Beverage Control, Marine Resources Police, State Capitol Police, Hospital Police, Park Police, Fish and Game Authorities, Water Police, Airport Police, Park Police, Mental Health Police, Natural Resources Police, fifty state Departments of Public Safety, U.S. Border Patrol, EPA police, Department of Agriculture Police, Immigration and Naturalization Police and the National Association of School Crossing Guards, are on the lookout for any sign of the missing woman.

"This is serious business and no effort will be spared to find former Secretary Clinton. Let me be clear," says the lame duck president Barack Obama in a TV news conference (no questions allowed from reporters), thinking as he reads the words from the teleprompter how much he dislikes that nasty woman who deserved whatever hand fate dealt her, and how convinced he is that Karma is at play here. No one deserves this more than Hillary Clinton. She is the Administration's own friggin' traitorous Private Bergdahl, chomping on the hand that fed her, switching from friend to foe.

At the same time, at the new Find Hillary Task Force Headquarters, some explanation of what happened is due the American public. So explanations are staged. Phrases thrown out to the media about the successful but dastardly kidnapping itself, like "brilliantly executed" and "thoroughly professional" are masks disguising what the

FBI already suspects – that this was a stunningly simple operation whether it had been carried out by seasoned professionals or rank amateurs.

Undoubtedly, senior officers agree, there was some amount of luck involved, but Hillary's detail had been operating far below the standards and norms expected. A cursory review by the Service reveals that the detail hadn't been tested or evaluated in quite some time. It is not something they want made public.

In sum, lapses in procedure had allowed the highest profile woman in America to be kidnapped. And neither the Secret Service nor anyone in Federal law enforcement has the slightest intention of letting those frigging so-far-unknown assailants get away with it. Every rock will be flipped, every basement corner searched, every suspicious car stopped, every telephone call and email monitored – a 'balls out' effort will be made. Law enforcement is going to do whatever it takes to get Hillary back alive, within the rules or without, laws or no laws. They will strive to keep law bending hidden and covered.

Everyone in the U.S. Government from the top down knows that the longer the woman is missing, the more inept they all look. "Stumbling, bumbling fools" is how one radio talk show host is already describing them. They also know that whoever plays the biggest role in finding her, particularly alive, will not only get national acclaim, but the kind of media adulation that opens Congressional budget coffers. Nothing succeeds like success, and everyone within that nascent Task Force wants a bigger piece of any pie to slide out from the ovens of Uncle Sugar's kitchen.

Within twenty-four hours of her kidnapping, the Find Hillary Task Force Operations Center has been put together on the third and fourth floors of a building on G Street, Northwest, just east of the White House.

The space was on the market for lease and although it has virtually none of the amenities or special requirements needed for a high-profile office or classified operations center, it is a convenient location for the White House, the Department of Justice, and the FBI. It is also close to the Metro Center Metro Station, giving it easier access for departments and agencies headquartered further away from the center of town.

Representatives of the Department of Justice, the FBI, Homeland Security, the Secret Service, the Pentagon, the military services, the CIA, the Defense Intelligence Agency, the D.C. Police Department, the National Security Agency, the Joint Special Operations Command in Fort Bragg, North Carolina, state police from Maryland, Virginia, West Virginia and Pennsylvania, local law enforcement agencies from counties extending outward from the District, the Capital Police, the Naval Investigative Service, and liaison representatives from each of the various other states across the country will initially man the center. Other, specialized organizations and more robust state presences will be included if the effort goes on over time. For now, the belief is that Hillary is likely hidden somewhere along the Eastern seaboard.

In a slower moving endeavor, the new offices would have required special construction in the walls, ceilings and floors to meet the necessities of working with top secret material - information that would have come from sophisticated technical collection platforms such as those NSA or CIA uses, or from confidential sources whose identify needed to be protected. The building would also have needed special communications requirements for the passing of similarly sensitive material.

But this is about Hillary, and every minute invested is crucial. There was no time to build anything 'special', and the White House waived all standard high-level security requirements. Controlling ingress/egress is a means of controlling access to or use of top-secret material. Consideration about moving to a more secure, appropriately configured facility will only be given if the drama drags on.

Much that transpires is unclassified. As soon as telephone banks are installed, operators brought in from other government agencies, and phone numbers given to the general public to report tips or suspicious activity, the avalanche of routine information begins.

If something appears to develop it will then become "sensitive," and if a law enforcement response is being put together it will become "highly sensitive." This is mostly to keep it from the media, though so many warm bodies are involved leaks will be almost impossible to contain and prevent.

Besides NSA's monitoring of Facebook, Twitter, and Instagram, local law enforcement is put on alert by federal authorities and encouraged to monitor the same social media. Smaller police agencies have become adept at using them to solve local crimes.

Prohibitions on NSA tracing and eavesdropping on domestic telephone calls and emails without a court order are set aside, pronto. The White House orders this, content to plead its case through the Solicitor General after the fact. Accordingly, NSA starts tracking calls or emails with certain key words in them, although the standard words such as "Hillary" or "kidnapping" or "reward" or "hostage" are quickly dropped from the list, since virtually everyone is using them while talking or emailing about her disappearance.

A highly sophisticated intelligence fusion center is immediately considered, based on a variation of a program used in Iraq to identify and target insurgents - CALEB, created by former Army intelligence specialists, could take thousands of pieces of disparate information or intelligence and, in effect, paint an accurate picture with them.

"Link analysis" is the term used to describe what it did. Its resultant products were matched up with operators who then conducted the operations that killed or captured the targeted individual in a manner much like the raid that killed bin-Laden.

The program had been so successful, particularly given the massive amounts of data that it had to analyze, that it seems a natural for the search for Hillary. A problem loomed ahead with certainty: If she isn't found quickly the huge stream of information coming in from every conceivable source will overwhelm the ability of analysts and could crash the system.

The notion of technology solutions quickly brings out the private contractor crowd, intent on capitalizing on Hillary's misfortune. The winner out of the blocks is CGI Federal, the White House favorite for the failed Obamacare website. Despite their previous dismal performance, after being paid $678 million based on a sole-source, non-competitive contract – much of the money wasted - they have now won a contract with DHS. Known as the EAGLE II contract, it was competitive in appearance but had wired provisions which allowed CGI to again submit proposals for sole-source, non-competitive work. Once again the White House connections pay off – a few well-placed phone calls from Michelle Obama's Chief of Staff, one of her 137 personal but tax-payer funded employees, and doors open. It is, after all, in support of finding Hillary. Who can argue about timing or process?

Within 24 hours of submitting a proposal to "provide advanced mission-enabling technical solutions" to DHS in support of the multi-agency effort to find Hillary, CGI meets with DHS's senior contracting officer who then hand delivers a sole-source contract justification to the Department's General Counsel, gets his signature for approval, and issues a contract.

Chapter Eleven

By the second day, toll free telephone numbers for the public have been announced on every radio and TV station and every newspaper in the country, taking the burden off of local police and law enforcement emergency numbers which have been so inundated with calls that it is difficult to get through. The 9-11 call centers in the Washington metropolitan area are so overwhelmed that emergency callers attempting, for instance, to report serious crimes - murders, rapes, robberies, auto accidents and the like - are unable to get through, some experiencing busy signals on a dozen straight calls. Or half hour delays. At least two deaths may have been caused by the lack of emergency services response.

As expected, the initial hundreds of tips soon become thousands, every one of which has to be evaluated. Police telephones never seem to stop ringing.

Hillary is spotted on Interstate 95 North headed towards Baltimore in a 1969 Plymouth with Delaware plates at the exact same time she is spotted on Interstate 95 South in a red Acura with Maryland plates headed towards Richmond.

Sometimes a quick telephone conversation throws sufficient doubt on the tipster's story to simply record the call and move to the next one. Sometimes a call prompts a referral to a more experienced investigator. There is pervasive fear among the task force operators that some clue to Hillary's whereabouts might be overlooked in the rush and confusion of information.

Within hours she is seen in the passenger seat of a new white Mercedes with an old Romney/Ryan bumper sticker on the San Diego Freeway in Los Angeles. Moments later she is spotted in a wheezing, faded blue Ford pick up truck on Interstate 10 out near Phoenix, wearing a serape – "Yes, Ma'am. She had blonde hair. She was riding in the back with two tethered goats and a black dog. She was peering over the side and looked scared," says the caller. While it seems unlikely that she was transported so far so fast anything is considered possible.

One caller in a big rig headed down I-81 towards Roanoke, Virginia, makes a 9-11 call that is patched through to Washington. He gives his credentials as a former Hackensack, New Jersey, police officer. He is serious, business-like and rational. He is a big Hillary fan and says that he is playing "cat and mouse" with a white Ford Expedition, couple years old, Maryland plates, in which Hillary is in the passenger seat.

He reads the plate number loudly. A big, dark haired guy was driving. The trucker likes Hillary and has seen her on television a hundred times. "It's her," he says, excitedly. "I'm certain of it." He'd been working private security once on the Jersey shore, and had seen her up-close when she attended a fundraiser in Sommers Point at the famous old rock and roll bar called Tony-Marts.

In response to questions barked by a detective at the command post in Washington, to whom the call has been transferred, he says, "No, she doesn't look like she is restrained. She was drinking out of a soft drink bottle a minute ago." In fact she had looked just up at him and smiled as the car passed him on the left in the fast lane. He had been able to watch her face for at least four or five seconds from a distance of 10 or 12 feet, he tells them. "It's her," he reiterates. "I know it is." He's accelerating and catching up, he says.

The detective patches him through to a console in the actual operations center. An FBI agent and two Homeland Security intelligence specialists listen as his voice crackles through a speaker. "I'm catching up again. Jeez, they are going fast. I'm in the right lane. I'm at mile marker 167."

A plate search is immediately initiated while the agents listen. Calls are placed to Virginia State Police to converge on the area and prepare for a take down. The FBI's rapid response team at Quantico is alerted. The driver sounds convincing and convinced. He gives his own truck description and information so the police will know he is part of what's going down.

"I'm pulling alongside. I can see her again just ahead of me. I think the driver is slowing down a bit. I'm looking down. She's looking up. Oh my God," he blurts out. There is a long pause. The agents are leaning on the console in anticipation.

"What is it, man? Is it her?" says the FBI agent.

"Well," says the trucker, thoroughly chagrined, "I was looking down when she pulled up her top and flashed her boobs at me. She was laughing. I guess it wasn't Hillary Clinton, after all. Sorry."

"We're sorry too," says the FBI agent as the phone goes dead.

Other calls are equally off base though not as detailed or as lengthy. Hillary is spotted in diners, malls, theaters, gas stations, trailer parks, campgrounds, and neighbors' houses up and down the East Coast. One caller sees her at a homeless shelter in Baltimore. Another watches her praying in a back pew in a small Methodist church in Johnstown, Pennsylvania. Another watches two Muslim men sneaking something heavy under a sheet into a local Mosque. Convinced it is Hillary, the woman calls local authorities who immediately go to investigate. It's a side of beef stolen from a Safeway frozen food truck.

Another caller sees Hillary on the back of a motorcycle in Georgia with a small man wearing a Hells Angels jacket. Someone else is convinced he saw her on a bicycle on the W&OD Trail near Purcellville, Virginia, with a golden retriever trotting alongside.

For the most part, the callers are well meaning. A few want to find out what the reward is for inside skinny leading to her rescue. Some are disappointed to learn that no reward has yet been decided upon. Others simply hang up abruptly when they are informed. But a substantial reward *is* being considered - a very large reward, not just from wealthy supporters and admirers of Hillary, but from the Bill, Hillary and Chelsea Clinton Foundation, which has more money than the national treasuries of at least fifty member nations of the United Nations: $10 million in reward money is the amount being discussed.

The promise of a huge money award for her safe return adds to the allure of getting her back. But it isn't just money that draws people. Fame, power, prestige, public adulation, book offers – the other rewards are significant and appealing. While many people are genuinely concerned about Hillary, others are already fantasizing about what it will mean to them personally if they are involved in her rescue.

Chapter Twelve

Mildred Paperman is feeling every bit her age, which is 69. Her legs ache and her feet hurt. Diabetic nerve pain, she is certain – cable TV ads for the condition make this clear to her, though she has been a Type 2 diabetic for only a few months, after she added some weight to her short, slightly squat frame.

Well, anyway, she would have said to her sister Devorah, with whom she shares a tiny house, that she feels like shit scraped off the bottom of a shoe. But Devorah isn't around to listen. She is off on one of her Alaskan cruises with her latest, crazy Samoan boyfriend, and won't be back for a week, so Mildred will have to keep her complaints to herself.

She wanders past the pickup trucks parked in a row, bulging with fruit and corn and other vegetables at the Farmers Market in the small Maryland burg of Darden, not far from her home in Rockville, about 20 miles from Washington, D.C. It is a balmy Tuesday morning, one day after Hillary Clinton was kidnapped.

Mildred notices that three or four produce truck radios are tuned to WTOP, the Washington all news station, their volumes up as correspondents' reports about the search for Mrs. Clinton are broadcast.

She hears two right wing pontificators, (RWP's she calls them) chattering about the kidnapping on a show called Danger Zone. Carlson and Cowan are their names. They have actually characterized this heinous, horrible crime with the flippant name, "Snatching Hillary."

They are generally rude and disrespectful men. Just another couple of media knuckleheads, she thinks. She has heard them before, making fun of public servants and hard-working politicians. She hates the pair. She sometimes carps about them at her League of Women Voters meetings.

But Mildred loves Hillary, a fighter for women, she believes, a defender of the female underdog, with whom Mildred identifies. Too bad that whoever did this hadn't grabbed Hillary's pig of a husband instead.

Typical, even in kidnappings women get the short end of the stick. Look at Patty Hearst, she thinks. They kidnapped Patty and her boyfriend Steven Weed together but let Weed, who was really a wet noodle, go in a day. They kept Patty for months. So unfair.

Mildred is carrying a cloth bag with handles, $1.50 at Whole Foods, and has already filled it with four beefsteak tomatoes and a half dozen medium size zucchini, which, titillating truth be told, reminded her, firm and smooth and not aggressively large, of the schvantz of her old boss, and lover of 30 years, Bernie Kovacs.

She looks into the face of the vegetable seller, a young man with hair over his ears, as she strokes a zucchini before placing it gently in her bag. That boy would never, ever, in a million years, imagine that this reserved old lady is having a lewd flashback, however momentary.

It is then that Mildred drops her green tote bag and follows it to the ground, flattening the tomatoes, and settling silently in a heap, being poked in the thigh by a zucchini (just as Bernie used to sometimes do during their nap time) after a blood clot breaks loose from its perch on the wall of her carotid artery and collides, with devastating impact, against the right side of her brain.

In Boca Raton, Florida, Bernie Kovacs is sitting under his new electric "Sun Setter Awning" on the back deck of his condo when his wife hands him the ringing phone through a kitchen window.

Mrs. Kovacs is glad for the phone respite as Bernie insisted on playing with the Sun Setter remote, trying to open and close the awning in three minutes or less (as the salesman had claimed it would) causing a whirring sound in the kitchen, where she is trying to watch General Hospital on ABC, a soap-opera to which she has been addicted for more than 30 years.

Bernie is grateful that she ducked back inside as he recognizes Mildred's voice, as odd as it sounds, and whatever this call is about he doesn't want to have to explain it to the missus, who had always been suspicious of his relationship with Mildred in the many decades she had worked at his Rockville, Maryland, paper box factory, before they had both retired.

Bernie hasn't talked with Mildred in over a year. He still cares about her though, even after the sparks had extinguished, and, as she can barely speak, she puts a nurse at the emergency hospital on the phone to explain the stroke. And the phone call.

Bernie says he will fly up that afternoon and help get her moved to a temporary facility until she can enter serious rehab, which the nurse says she will definitely need.

Bernie then calls a friend who is the absentee owner of a string of nursing homes, one of which, Tarry Awhile, is in Rockville, Maryland. He makes off-the-books arrangements, for cash, for a two week stay, explaining that he needs to remain anonymous as Mildred Paperman is an old girlfriend. He then tells his wife he has business in Washington, changes clothes, packs a small suitcase, and heads for the airport.

Chapter Thirteen

Lucille Hamburger is the night RN at the Tarry Awhile facility. She was suspicious about the blonde woman patient in the private room right from the get-go. She is suspicious about many things in life, sometimes wrongly she realizes, but this has genuine traction. The owner of the home lives in Florida and visits only occasionally. He is a stranger to most of the staff. Lucille has only met him once in her six years in the Tarry Trenches.

And it is the owner who has passed word to the home's administrator that the new patient, a Miss Paperman, is a stroke victim and will only stay for a week or ten days before she is transferred to a rehab facility. She has been paid for in advance, there is to be no record of her stay, and she is not to be disturbed. Nor is the man sometimes visiting her. He is to be left alone.

"It is really unusual," thinks Lucille Hamburger. "Way out of sync." This new patient is semi-comatose and to be tube fed only through a cut down in her chest. Her arms are tied with restraints to the hospital bed rails as she becomes intermittently agitated. The bedside visitor, an elderly man in therapeutic crepe-soled shoes, wants to remain anonymous. "What is going on here?"

"Well, he sure does want to be anonymous," thinks Miss Hamburger, as she watches him sitting in the patient's room, wearing a cheap wig and oversized sunglasses. "Mr.

No Name," she calls him to herself. He is clearly up to No Good.

After the man leaves, Lucille Hamburger wanders down the hall and peers into the room. The patient is snoring loudly. Miss Hamburger hovers over her, studying her face, a face she is sure she has seen somewhere before.

Duh, no wonder she knows the face - it belongs to Hillary Clinton, one of the most famous women in the world and now a crime victim. "Holy Mother of God!" Lucille whispers to herself.

Why would she be here? Maybe she didn't have a stroke. Maybe she is being kept in a drugged state and is being parked here for a short stay, like some stolen car at a chop shop, as her police friends call them. Hidden here until the story fades off the front page with the connivance of that awful man who owns this place and his buddy, Mr. No Name in the road-kill wig, who must be one of her kidnappers.

Lucille Hamburger slides her iPhone from the pocket of her starched white uniform – the only employee in the whole facility not to wear cheap scrub pajamas to work every day. She turns on the reading light over the head of the sleeping woman and takes two photos of her face.

She will call her friend at the Montgomery County Sheriff's Office, Lt. Kelly. She is so excited she thinks she might wet her pants.

Lt. "Clam Box" Kelly's first name is Peter. He had picked up the handle Clam Box in his youth. He is sitting at his desk picking his teeth and looking at a newspaper.

Peter Kelly grew up in the working class beach town of Revere, Massachusetts, about five miles north of Boston. His parents owned a tiny joint on the boardwalk called Kelly's Clam Box - four stools and a counter.

Young Peter spent summers working 12-hour shifts as a Clam Box fry cook, living on fried whole belly clams, clam cakes, clam chowder and bottles of Moxie, a cola made since after the Civil War in the nearby town of Lowell from caramel flavoring, spring water and gentian root – a slightly bitter drink believed to boost both energy and physical courage. ("That fella has a lot of moxie," folks would say.) Moxie was endorsed in radio ads by Clam Box Kelly's hero, Boston Red Sox slugger Ted Williams.

Clam Box has enjoyed a leisurely, and free, Denny's Big Breakfast and is about to read the latest Washington Post front page news about the kidnapping of the Clinton woman, when his phone beeps, signaling the arrival of a message. He sees that he has a text. It's from that scary head nurse at the Tarry Awhile nursing home. He deals with her about once a month when a patient wanders away, usually to be found sitting alone on a bus stop bench.

There is a message and a photo attached. "Is this Mrs. Clinton?" it says. "If so, she is being hidden in our nursing home. Her kidnapper has her drugged and comes in for two hours every afternoon to watch her."

Clam Box stares at the photo, eyes widening. The picture does look like her. If this is really Hillary, my God, we will be international heroes here at the substation. Holy Shit, if I handle this right I could end up running the frigging Maryland State Police.

Clam Box can hardly contain himself.

He grabs his hat, hoists his Sam Browne belt over his belly, makes a reassuring adjustment to his holstered 9mm Glock and heads for the door. He drives straight home, not to the nursing home. His wife is at work and the apartment is empty. He changes into a sport jacket, golf shirt and slacks in 15 minutes and is out the door – on his way to get a first hand look at this broad in bed at the Tarry Awhile.

.

Chapter Fourteen

Within hours of the kidnapping, thousands of pundits, commentators and all-purpose chattering heads – a teeming gaggle the size of an entire U.S. Army Division, on staff or on contract to every TV and cable network, every American political and news website, from the right to the left: the Daily Caller, Drudge, The Hill, Politico, The Huffington Post, The Daily Kos, Weekly Standard, Slate, Salon, Breitbart, Town Hall, Front Page, Newsmax, Lucianne, Red State, The Washington Examiner, The Blaze, Firedoglake, Truthdig, PJ Media, Michelle Malkin, The Democratic Underground, National Review, Indy Media, The Nation, Planned Parenthood Blog, Feministing, Liberal Logic, The World Socialists and The American Prospect, to name a few and omit hundreds of others; plus editorial and opinion writers for every North American newspaper, large and small, daily and weekly, and from more than 60 countries on every continent, are all laboring to establish their bona fides as terrorism experts.

This is a likely case of terrorism. At least that's what the world, at first blush, is being led to believe, with no evidence other than past experience, and some common sense, to support that view.

No one is blaming radical Islam, not so far, and operatives from the Congress for American-Islamic Relations (CAIR) are calling around to newsrooms to make sure that doesn't happen, or dropping accusations on the doorsteps of home-grown right wingers, who are being broadly suggested as terrorists by leftwingers. The fact is, no one has a clue as to who did this or why they did it or where Hillary is.

The woman was crazy-famous before she was kidnapped.

A survey two years earlier, in February 2014, showed how obsessed the media was with Hillary. And this was well before she announced that she would run for the presidency again. In one 48-hour period, Hillary was mentioned in the U.S. media 124,000 times, according to Google. In one week CNN devoted 72 minutes of news time to her while MSNBC dwelled on Hillary and the "War on Women" for a total of 57 minutes of airtime. Even Fox News gave her 44 minutes in one week. Small wonder she is so famous.

Two days after the kidnapping in 2016, in just a 24-hour period, mentions of Hillary in news stories worldwide number well in excess of 10 million.

"It defies belief that someone could pull this off so professionally," writes David Ignatius in the Washington Post. "This was as well planned and executed as any successful terrorist act." Posted in Beirut in the '70's, Ignatius has lived the 'terrorism experience' and is viewed as highly credible by his readers.

"One of the most professional terrorist actions we've ever witnessed," opines Peter Bergen, CNN's prime terrorism expert. "We may trace this back to the senior leadership of ISIS."

Bergen's credibility is sometimes iffy. He had initially claimed in April, 2012, that the Boston Marathon Bombers were right-wing extremists. The murderous Tsarnaev brothers, Dzhokhar and the now-deceased Tamerlan, were soon shown to be anti-American Islamist transplants from Chechnya.

Various retired big-city homicide detectives, retired FBI officers, former CIA paramilitary officers and analysts, joined by retired military officers through the rank of four-star general, have popped up like shooting gallery ducks on all the major networks and cable news shows. Their views fall into a general consensus pool: the kidnapping was probably a professional operation, probably committed by terrorists.

Fourteen years earlier, many of the very same TV talkers had claimed that the ubiquitous and deadly D.C. sniper was a white man, probably with an extensive military background: little question in their minds.

In fact, the snipers were a pair of homeless black men living in their beat-up Chevy Caprice and firing randomly from a perch in its trunk. The two were linked to al-Qaeda about as closely as your Aunt Maude.

Unknown to every talking head, media pontificator and senior executive and investigator from a dozen acronymic federal law enforcement agencies, Wayne B. Wayne and Billy "Zipper" Fly, the men who kidnapped Hillary Clinton and who are now holding her prisoner in the basement of an upper-class Washington, D.C., home, are two Texas country boys of normal intelligence but limited sophistication; utterly without ideological or political views except on the most fundamental, patriotic level.

They had a little earlier military training it is true, or one did, and certainly some level of self discipline to assist in plans and the execution of them, but nothing extraordinary.

As boys, and they aren't much more than boys now, they were nice to their parents, kind to children and small animals, polite to strangers, and mostly respectful to women.

They have pulled off a stunning kidnapping that grabbed the attention of the entire *world* and it has nothing whatsoever to do with an experiential skill-set, or covert ops experience, or steely ideologically fed determination. It has *everything* to do with simple good luck - serendipity out of control, you could say.

Chapter Fifteen

In retrospect, particularly given that Hillary was unharmed and reasonably well treated, luck was indeed the guiding handmaiden in their success.

The précis of the FBI's subsequent investigation into the backgrounds of the two kidnappers is mundane - nothing special about either of them.

> *Wayne Brad Wayne, 33 (born August 17, 1983, at Denton County, Texas General Hospital), grew up on a small farm near Frisco, Texas. His father was Brad Wayne. His mother was the former Sue Ann Grimes. Both parents were born and raised in the Collin County, Texas, area. Their farm produced large amounts of feed corn and hay and appears to have been financially successful. Brad Wayne and Sue Ann Wayne still live and work there. They have so far refused to be interviewed by the Bureau.*

> *Wayne Wayne has one sibling, Mrs. Carol Wayne Simpson of Fort Worth, Texas, who has also refused to be interviewed by the FBI.*

> *In the spring of 2001, at 18, Wayne graduated from Frisco High School where he played football. He was a linebacker. (There is such intense interest in the game that a "Go Raccoons" banner hangs*

across Main Street in Frisco during football season.)

According to interviews with former classmates, Wayne Wayne was well liked but was quiet and considered shy.

School records reflect a general grade point average of C for academic classes (English, History, etc.) and somewhat higher grades, A's and B's, in shop courses like Carpentry, Principles of Electricity, and Auto Engine Repair. His Stanford-Binet IQ score was 109, above the national average for white males. He did not take the ACT or SAT College Board tests. He told his school counselor that he intended to join the military and later to seek law enforcement work in Texas.

Miss (name redacted) of Dallas was the girlfriend of Wayne Wayne for the last two years of high school, 1999 to 2001, until his military enlistment. In an interview with FBI agents she described Wayne as even-tempered, considerate and very likeable. She had known him as a classmate and friend since the 6th grade.

She admitted to a sexual relationship with Wayne through the final months of their senior school year in 2001. She was not previously sexually experienced (and did not think that Wayne was either) and described him as "completely normal" and free of perversions and fetishes.

She has not been in contact with Wayne Wayne since he joined the military and she left Frisco for college in another part of the state. She did say she received a Christmas card from him a few years ago, forwarded by her mother, and that the photo on the card showed that he was married with two children.

Wayne Wayne enlisted in the U.S. Army on June 10, 2001, two weeks after high school graduation. The recruiter was MSgt Rosalie Benti at the Joint Military Recruitment Center in Dallas/Fort Worth. Master Sgt Benti, now retired, was contacted at her home in Conway, Arkansas but could not recall Wayne Brad Wayne.

Wayne Brad Wayne's four-year military record was unremarkable but honorable. He suffered no disciplinary actions or proceedings, graduated from ten weeks of Basic Combat Training at Fort Benning, Georgia, and was assigned to Military Police training.

Wayne was rated a Marksman with both the Colt .45 pistol and the M4 carbine and was later given the Army Good Conduct medal. He attended the U.S. Army Military Police School at Fort Leonard Wood, Missouri, and graduated in the approximate middle of his class from the 20-week course.

He was then promoted from Private E-2 to PFC (E-3) (he had been promoted automatically to E-2 upon completion of Basic Training) and assigned to the U.S. Army base in Sembach, Germany, in February, 2002, as a Military Policeman with the 92nd MP Battalion where some of his fellow enlisted men dubbed him 'Wayne Squared' for his often strait-laced behavior and his name, Wayne Wayne.

Note: The Army Military Police maintain law, order, discipline and security for U.S. Army personnel. The Motto of their Police School is "Of the Troops, For the Troops."

Military Police soldiers are recognized as law enforcement professionals and offer anti-terrorism and force-protection specialists to handle crimes committed on Army installations. Wayne's service records reflect no MP specialties beyond basic criminal law enforcement and traffic control.

Wayne Wayne spent 28 months at the Sembach base in Germany and was transferred to the garrison at Fort Hood, Texas (near Waco), where he was a base MP until his honorable discharge in May, 2005, with the rank of sergeant E-5.

Wayne Wayne, then 22, moved back to his parents' home in Frisco. He worked on their farm for six months and then obtained a position with the Hyde, Texas, township as a sworn constable (one of three), where he remained, without incident, for three years, before joining the store security staff at the Walmart store back in Frisco.

He married the former Rae Ann Cummings (born in Brenham, Texas, Oct 21, 1985) in Hyde, Texas, in June, 2006. She joined him in the move to Frisco with their two young children in August, 2008.

Wayne Wayne was promoted to Loss-Prevention Supervisor at the Walmart in Frisco in 2012. The following year his wife left him (reportedly for another man) and moved to Dallas. They subsequently divorced. Rae Anne Wayne, now Rae Anne Gilbert, has not been available for an FBI interview and is uncooperative on the telephone.

Wayne B. Wayne is very active in the Masonic Lodge of Frisco, located at 4000 Wazoo Rd, within the city limits, according to Mr. (redacted) and Mr. (redacted) both longtime Frisco members. This is part of the Grand Lodge of Texas, Ancient Free and Accepted Masons (AF & AM) as they term themselves, founded in 1838. It has 889 other lodges in the state and 105,000 members. It is the 5th largest Masonic Grand Lodge in the world.

Neither Frisco Lodge member interviewed divulged any deleterious information about Wayne Wayne. They each said he was a very energetic member and had achieved the status of "32nd degree Mason," the highest level of membership accorded, and thusly had been admitted to the Shriner's Lodge. They said he was now entitled to wear a red tasseled fez and that a fez had been presented to him by his lodge brothers.

Loring Battle, manager of the Walmart in Frisco, described Wayne Brad Wayne as an "excellent" employee, "earnest and hard working and so far as we ever knew, very honest." Ms. Battle said she was shocked by the public allegations against Wayne. She did say that the divorce from his wife and the loss of his children - Mrs. Wayne took their only vehicle and their pets, as well - seemed to have had a serious negative effect on Wayne Wayne. He was "more remote and reserved, for certain," she said. "He seemed very unhappy."

Wayne resigned his security position with Walmart the week before Christmas, 2015, and gave just ten days notice, leaving officially on January 3rd.

His co-workers were surprised, as he was popular with management and seemed destined for further advancement in the security area. He declined a going-away party and said he was "going to be looking for new opportunities – and some adventure, perhaps back east somewhere."

Chapter Sixteen

Zipper's story was somewhat different. According to the FBI report,

William Paris Fly was born May 16, 1991, at his mother's home on the Arkansas side of the city of Texarkana, Arkansas (it is divided in two parts, with the other half in Texas.)

In 1991, the total population of Texarkana was about 50,000 people.

William Fly's father, William London Fly, (born Feb 3, 1963) was a prison guard at the Texarkana Regional Correction Center in Arkansas. (If there is any significance to the father and son's middle names it is not known.)

William P. Fly's mother was Sadie (NMI) Snarker, (born April 12, 1975). She turned age 16 a month before her son's birth. The parents were unmarried. The mother was a clerk at the Centre Street, Texarkana, Arkansas, Piggly Wiggly store until the final week of her pregnancy in 1991. She dropped out of the Daisy Jones Middle School in Texarkana, Arkansas, at the end of the 8th grade, two years before.

The father and mother resided together, with the baby, at the Texarkana, Texas, Motel 8 for the remainder of 1991, until January, 7, 1992, when William London Fly was arrested by FBI agents

and officers from the Arkansas State AG's office. They charged him with aiding a female inmate, one Gloria Borger, 22, to escape. Borger was captured within a day of her flight. (She had hidden in a prison laundry truck. She immediately implicated Fly, with whom, she said, she had been having sex.)

Fly was convicted and on March 5, 1992, he was sentenced to twenty years to life, to be served in the prison where he had been a guard. He was murdered there by another prisoner after a fight over the affections of a female guard on Feb 10, 1998.

Sadie Snarker married Waldo Brenner (born July 5, 1968), no criminal record, a roofer from Tony's Township, Arkansas, in 1996. The pair moved to Frisco, Texas, in the following month, with the boy, William Paris Fly, then 5 years of age.

As of this writing, Sadie Snarker Brenner and Waldo Brenner are still married. They own a small roofing company in Frisco, employing four fulltime employees with Mrs. Brenner running the company office. They are well thought of by a half dozen neighbors who were questioned. No derogatory information was offered about the family. They did refuse to discuss her son William Paris Fly with agents.

William Paris Fly, known as Billy and also nicknamed Zipper (apparently a schoolboy *reference to his surname, Fly) attended grammar, middle and high school in Frisco. He has no arrest record. He received good grades at Frisco HS and graduated in the class of 2009, having maintained a B average. His Stanford-Binet IQ was relatively high - 119.*

He played second-string football but was never large enough or aggressive enough to make the first team, said two different classmates. He restored a 1949 Ford convertible, purchased by funds he saved from various part-time and summer jobs. He had a reputation as being very good with automobiles and other mechanical devices.

Billy Fly apparently won an informal but competitive athletic competition of some kind in his last year at Frisco High School. Details are not known. There is some mystery about this and the event in question may have sexual connotations. Three possible reportees, all former classmates, were contacted but none seemed sure of what the competition actually was, or if they did know they would not say. All were warned that it is unlawful to lie to a federal law enforcement officer.

William Paris Fly does not seem to have been known to Wayne Brad Wayne at Frisco High School, as they were so many years apart.

Fly attended the Collin County Community College for two years after high school, maintaining grades good enough for his transfer to Texas A & M, to which he was accepted in 2010.

For unknown reasons, Fly failed to enroll in college and went to work at his parents' company as a roofer for three years before taking a part time job with Walmart and their Garden & Yard Center in 2012, when and where he became acquainted with and then friendly with Wayne B. Wayne. Various interviewees said the men were close friends and that they knew each other from around town, and from their employment at Walmart. "They liked each other," said one man, Mr.(name redacted) a fellow employee at Walmart, "but Wayne Wayne was the leader of the two."

William Paris Fly quit his job at Walmart on January 1, 2016, two days before Wayne Wayne's resignation became effective. Fly does not seem to have told anyone, including his parents, where he was going or what he had planned to do. He disappeared immediately thereafter.

Chapter Seventeen

Zipper and Wayne pack Zipper's dark blue 1949 Ford convertible with its white cloth top and flathead V-8 engine with a couple of duffel bags of clothes and gear, plus two sleeping bags for emergencies, though they have plenty of cash to pay for motels for their 1400 mile cross country drive.

Zipper won't be driving the old Ford for long, regardless of sentimentality, its nifty appearance and its basic reliability. Like a good looking but totally senile old fellow it has outlived its social usefulness and it is time for God to take it home. In this case, the metaphorical God is Wally White himself at Wally White's Carrollton, Texas, Classic Cars.

Wally has said on the phone that if the car is in as good shape as Zipper represented, and the title and papers are tiptop as well, he will take it and hand over a cashier's check for $15,000. They head north on the Dallas Toll Road and in the late morning drive into Carrollton.

The Auto Sales Row is only a few blocks long. Zipper drives right past Wally White's and turns into another establishment entirely: the Lone Star Motors sales lot. He drops Wayne at the lot entrance. It is 11am. "Pick me up at Wally's in one hour," he says, and drives off.

A man is waiting for Wayne inside the tiny office. As Wayne closes the flimsy door behind him the man stands next to a desk, and says, "Ah, Mr. Benson, Floyd Benson. Right on time. I'm the fella who talked to you yesterday. Hector is the name, great deals is my game. And you are going to be happy with this one, my friend."

"I am *already* happy, Hector," says Wayne. And he is. "Everything gets better from here."

For an all cash deal, as Wayne has offered on the telephone, Hector has lowered the price on the premium black 2012 Chevrolet Suburban model 1500 from $29,500 to $27,500. In 15 minutes Hector's man has the temp plates and title transfer ready for Wayne.

Wayne produces his phony Floyd Benson Texas driver's license, with its Houston address, a battered social security card, and a black "Diamond Preferred" Citibank Master Card with a tiny picture of him on its corner. The picture, of course, isn't actually him but it doesn't matter. He isn't using it to buy anything. Wayne kept Benson's wallet after it had been turned in to Walmart's Lost & Found from the parking lot. Mr. Benson never came to or called Walmart and inquired about it. Wayne figured he might have some use for a fake ID someday.

Wayne pulls a white envelope from his trouser pocket. It is packed with 275 $100 bills, part of $50,000 in cash given him that morning by Earl "Fatha" Hines at the latter's

Frisco home when he and Zipper stopped by for coffee and final orders. The $50,000 is for immediate expenses.

Hector examines each bill with a pen device. When he finishes, he smiles, shakes Wayne's hand, and dangles two sets of car keys at him with the other.

The Suburban is black and sleek, freshly simonized. It has running boards, a rear view camera, cocoa-mahogany colored leather bucket seats in the front, and polished aluminum wheels. It is a 4-wheel drive V-8, miserable on gas consumption but quick on pickup. It has only 46,000 miles on it.

"Here is our full-on fucking Secret Service War Wagon," says Wayne to Zipper, as he picks him up by the curb at Wally White's. They sling their duffels, garment bags and sleeping bags into the back of the big Suburban, head out into traffic and began their trek to the nation's capitol and a rendezvous with Hillary Clinton.

Hours later they are doing well. No flat tires. No smoke roiling out of the exhaust. Windshield wipers working as they pass through a small rainstorm. Not much of interest to worry about, speaking automotively, as they make their way smoothly across the country.

A break in the routine comes when Zipper sees a Dairy Queen while passing alongside a frontage road.

"Dairy Queen, my all-time favorite," says Zipper, as he sees the 'Heath Bar Blizzard - any day' sign. They stop and buy two of them.

"Did you know they are calling some of the Dairy Queens 'DQ Grill and Chill'? No shit. 'Dairy Queens.' They thought it sounded like gay farmers." He is laughing. Both men feel good.

They are cruising two miles below the current limit of 70 mph, heading east on I-30 towards Memphis. Wayne is at the wheel and sets the speed at 68mph by cruise control. The Suburban handles nicely, not like a truck or even a big car, but smooth and effortless and powerful.

The Sirius/XM satellite radio service is free for thirty days, courtesy of Hector at Lone Star Motors. Wayne punches in channel 7, for some old-time music. Rick Nelson is singing "Garden Party," his early 70's hit about his disastrous appearance at Madison Square Garden with Chuck Berry, Bo Didley and Bobby Rydell. Nelson was singing his classic "Mary Lou" when he heard booing in the back of the huge crowd. It was directed against three uniformed cops who were struggling to arrest a druggie, but Nelson thought it was for him. He walked off the stage, not to return. Garden Party wafts through stereophonic speakers.

The demand by Fatha, at a long planning session, that Wayne and Zipper stay below the speed limit and commit no other traffic violations driving across the country, was part of a larger point he hammered home.

Said Fatha, "Rule Number One - do no harm, intentional or unintentional. Do nothing that will come back at you with its teeth flashing. Leave no fucking fingerprints, real or symbolically. No DNA, either, thank you."

"The Feds will start picking the entire country apart bit by bit looking for clues, trying to find that Suburban, examining the most diddly-squat things that might lead them to *you*. You do not want to help them. Think how you'd feel spending the rest of your life in prison because your stupidity put you there. Do nothing before or after your time in Washington to trigger any police interest, no matter how innocent or explainable. Do nothing that can be tracked back to you after the snatch goes down. That's how people get caught. Little, teeny things that draw attention. Some cop remembers pulling over two guys in a black Suburban with Texas plates driving through Virginia a few weeks back. He watched them as they rolled through a stop sign a little after leaving McDonalds and didn't make a full fucking stop. He pulled 'em over. They were polite and friendly, it was late, streets were empty, so he didn't give them a ticket. But, it turns out, he saved their license number or their physical description, or both, in his little notebook and went back and found it after his sergeant read a federal BOLO about the kidnapping of Mrs. Clinton at their shift meeting. Don't get stopped at all, for anything, I'm saying. And stay out of the fast lane."

Wayne pulls off at Texarkana and takes Broad Street into downtown, following a sign to the Subway sandwich shop. They park in front and bring their food to the car.

Across Broad Street at the corner of Stateline Avenue (Arkansas is a few yards away) is a billboard advertising the "Ball & Chain Golf Tournament" to benefit some prisoner programs at the Texarkana Regional Correctional Center, whose pile of multi-story buildings begins about 100 feet away, across the intersection.

Zipper looks out at the sprawling TRCC buildings.

"My dad used to work there," he says to Wayne. "He was a guard at that prison when I was born."

"Waldo was?" asks Wayne. "You lived here?"

"I don't remember it," says Zipper. "We left for Frisco when I was little. Waldo is my stepfather. My real father ran off. I don't remember him. He might have died. I don't know. My mother said she hasn't heard from him in 20 years, that maybe he left the country."

"How's that chicken pizzaiola sub?" Zipper asks. "I've always thought I would like one. I love Monterey cheddar."

They pull into Memphis about 7:30pm, having covered 275 miles in four hours and six minutes, sticking to the speed limit.

The store suggested by Fatha won't open until 9am the next day, so they drive past Graceland, Elvis Presley's old home, gawk at the knots of fans milling on the sidewalk, even on a winter night, and look for a motel.

There are dozens to pick from, as the neighborhood is overwhelmingly commercial: Roadside Inn, Super 8, Holiday Inn. There is a "vacancy" sign outside the 128-room Heartbreak Hotel, with its blonde 1950's furniture and heart shaped swimming pool and the decision is easy - a small suite is $138 a night for two, free coffee and Wi-Fi. Who could pass that up? The name alone is enough to get Wayne and Zipper up to their room

In the morning, they drive over to the store Fatha has told them about: Fun Magic, on South Highland Street across from the University of Memphis. The place is crammed with magic tricks and illusion devices, pranks, whoopee cushions, stink bombs, foaming soap, itching powder, exploding cigars and life size Bat Man costumes.

They walk out with two large plastic bags holding different caps and hats, eye glasses (horn rims and wire-rims, both with plain glass) makeup kits, putty, two wigs for men, one a dirty blonde, another, medium brown with a pony tail, and a very realistic rubber mask of Angelina Jolie, complete with long brown hair. Zipper pulls it over his head, takes a look in the mirror. It looks very real. He decides, for $49.95, he has to have it.

Two hefty black men in cargo shorts and Nike tennis shoes stop and are looking him over with suspicion. "It's not for me. It's for a lady friend," he says. "I'm gonna' make her wear it when we get it on." The men chuckle and Zipper laughs back. It is a joke but, in fact, he does have a planned use for it.

By 11pm they are in Front Royal, Virginia, 76 miles west of Washington, at the confluence of the North and South Forks of the Shenandoah River. They find a quiet motel, about to extinguish its office lights. Washington, D.C., is an hour and 15 minutes away, up Route 66.

It is a clear, crisp morning with a sky of cornflower blue featuring occasional puffs of stratocumulous clouds.

Zipper and Wayne have a leisurely breakfast at a happy looking little joint called The Daily Grind on Main Street in Front Royal. It offers WiFi and exotic coffee with a chalked menu on the wall. They share a pot of a 'strong and pithy' blend called "Jamaica Me Crazy" and a plate of blueberry bagels with ham and melted Stilton Cheese. It isn't Mickey D's but it is OK, thinks Zipper, who would have preferred McDonalds if they hadn't already hit so many over the past couple of days.

The added plus to the pleasant morning activities is finding a likely "Furnished House for Rent" on the internet in Washington's "Historic Georgetown Neighborhood," using the sleek silver-colored MacBook Pro given to them by Fatha.

The real estate Internet app Zillow informs them that the house on Dent Place, Northwest, is worth about $4 million. The Georgetown real estate broker offers a 25 scene virtual video internet tour of the house, showing every room and its minimal but attractive furnishings in color. It even has a picture of its large, immaculate garage, opening onto an alley to the rear. It plugs the location as "one block from the famous 3-story 'Red House' at 3321 Dent Place lived in by JFK and his sister Eunice (and a butler and cook) when Kennedy first became a congressman and moved to Washington in 1947."

The broker is asking for $8,000 a month, with a six-month to a one-year contract preferred.

Wayne and Zipper have spent a half-day at Fatha's house in Frisco being instructed on the Apple computer and the workings of apps like Zillow, Google, Google Earth, and others.

Wayne was already sufficiently computer literate; Zipper less so, though he quickly picked up on the easy-to-use Mac.

Wayne approaches the real estate office, a store front on P Street, in an effective disguise: a medium long men's blonde wig tucked under his tan Stetson cowboy hat, his cheeks puffed out by small clay inserts, clear glass horn rims in place.

Miss Sydney Bottomley, the friendly and socially proper owner of her solo agency - Bottomley's Fine Properties - is at her campaign desk, handed down from a dashing ancestor, Confederate General Rutherford "one-eye" Bottomley.

The man coming through the door has the look of a southerner. Miss Bottomley is instantly sympathetic.

Looking at the stranger, Miss Bottomley thinks the cowboy hat is acceptable, though he should have removed it as he approached her. He must be using it to hold that cheap wig in place. "Such a young fellow to be already bald. Sad," she thinks. With those cheeks he looks like her old hamster; his name was Bennie, and she loved him as a young girl. She can picture this fellow sitting on his haunches holding a Christmas walnut in his little paws.

She says, "Hello young man. How may I help you?"

The cover story, laid out for them by Fatha, works perfectly with Sydney Bottomley, like a hypnotist swinging a pendant. In this case, the pendant waved under her aquiline nose is a thick sheath of $100 dollar bills.

Wayne shows her his phony Houston driver's license. (She photocopies it later before she turns over the house keys.) He explains that he is the "advance man" and fulltime employee for a very successful, somewhat eccentric, oil tycoon from Houston. His boss has sent him ahead to scout a comfortable house for him and his wife to live in for a few weeks at the end of the month. They will be bringing a maid with them. The boss is planning on a series of lobbying visits to the Hill. The wife wants to tour museums. They are presently on their yacht in the Indian Ocean, somewhat incommunicado.

Wayne says he has worked for the oil man, a very rich "wildcatter," for more than a decade; and that the older man trusts his judgment. Wayne is authorized to spend more than $8,500 for a month's rent. Wayne takes out the large cash roll from a pocket in his blazer.

Miss Bottomley tries not to stare as he lays the pile on her desk. Wayne says, "I've seen your virtual tour and the house seems perfect. I'll give you $8,500 for a month," he is counting out the bills, "another $1,500 for a refundable damage deposit, and an extra $1,000 for *you* for your good service today, no record kept."

He put $10,000 in one pile and the $1,000 gift for Miss Bottomley beside it, tapping it with his index finger.

Wayne says, "When my boss and his wife get here in two weeks, I will bring them by your office to sign the papers, and to let you know whether they would like to extend the agreement for another month or two into the spring. He pays for everything with cash, so this is a good thing for everyone."

He says, "Here is my cell phone, if you need me," giving her the number of a disposable telephone he has purchased in Walgreen's drug store. "I'll be with the Old Man and his wife in two weeks or so. I'll be staying there alone until they come."

They shake hands at the door and Wayne walks down the block and round the corner. Zipper is sitting in the passenger seat. He is eating an ice cream cone from Thomas Sweets on the corner. Wayne dangles the keys to the house and the garage door opener, in a plastic sack. "All set," he says, chuckling. "Let's take us another look at the house on N Street for tomorrow."

The two have driven by the imposing gray house at 31st and N shortly after noon, when they first arrived in Washington.

They had found the gossip column item in "Reliable Sources" in the Style Section of the Washington Post two days before, at the hotel in Memphis. They check a Google search of new Hillary stories twice a day, and read the online versions of the Washington Times, The Washington Examiner and the Washington Post once a day.

This item said that the "PR Ace, Maxwell Brick, will be throwing a $10,000 a head fundraising fete for Hillary Clinton," giving the date in Georgetown, no specific address or time, but a phone number to call for tickets.

Finding Max Brick's N Street house address took less than five minutes on the Internet. A pretext phone call to the ticket number got them the time.

Wayne drives past the N Street house, eyeballing the front steps and door, turns up 31st Street and looks at the side door and gate and the two-car garage. He continues up 31st Street, using his auto GPS, and drives the six blocks to the alley behind the Dent Place house. He clicks open the garage doors, pulls in and shuts them behind him. After they unload their gear, Zipper pulls a set of D.C. license plates from the spare tire well. Two of four pair of Maryland, Virginia, and D.C. plates they had stolen from cars parked behind a New York Avenue Day's Inn motel that morning when they entered the city.

Chapter Eighteen

Metropolitan Police Officer Rodney B. Williams, a 26-year veteran of the D.C. police, is parked in his white squad car, with its red and blue painted flashes, in front of Billy Martin's Tavern, across from the beginning of N Street in Georgetown at the corner of Wisconsin Avenue.

Behind the lightly smoked windows he is chewing on a tuna fish and avocado sandwich and watching all the crazy media people unloading equipment from vans, scurrying around like big, pale insects in fancy clothes as they set up to do their reports.

The squad car is as battered and abused as a feral cat, but it is new to Rodney, who until a week ago had been the driver for Captain Stacey Kiester-Garcia, second in command of the police district – a masculine, heavy set blonde woman, known to the rank and file behind her muscular back as "Meester Kiester," pronounced *sotto voce* with an exaggerated Hispanic accent. Kiester is married to another police officer, Sgt. Alejandro Garcia, currently on the D.C. MPD Vice Squad.

Kiester-Garcia had never seemed to like Rodney in the year that he drove her unmarked gray Crown Vic, had seldom even spoken to him. After he turned from the front seat one night to hand her a full cup of steaming-hot Sonic Drive-In coffee ("served faster than the speed of sound") his elbow slipped and he poured ten ounces of it onto her crotch.

Now she really doesn't like him. Rodney had always assumed Captain Kiester-Garcia was physically tough. He was shocked by how loudly she cried and wailed on the way to the George Washington University Hospital's Emergency Room. Turned out she had third degree burns on her thighs and 'Lady's Unit' (as Rodney always called it.)

Captain Kiester-Garcia was convinced that Rodney had dropped the coffee on purpose, probably as an act of passive-aggression. When she returned to work after three days of medical leave, she drove herself to police headquarters on Indiana Avenue to see the Chief. The humiliation of having to walk with her thighs and unmentionable (as she always called it) wrapped in at least a pound of Vaseline-soaked gauze bandages made her feel murderous towards that stupid pig Officer Williams.

She was mortified as she waddled slowly down the hall of the Admin Building, suffering smirks and knowing looks from fellow police executives as she passed them. They'd all heard. The "Po-lice" grapevine knew everything and passed it on as fast as a Sonic coffee.

Chief Kathy Lanier claimed to be sympathetic about the burns, but she was not at all receptive to disciplining Officer Rodney B. Williams, whom she knew personally.

He had been one of her classmates at the Metropolitan Police Academy for 28 weeks – the famous, disastrous Class of 1989-90.

"Stacey, I'm sure it was just an accident. If he has a failing it is that he is not aggressive enough for a cop. Remove him as your driver, if you'd like, and just move him back to patrol."

N Street is roped off a block down, at the intersection of 31st and N, where the four-story mansion from which Hillary was kidnapped stands. The FBI and plainclothes police investigators are still interviewing neighbors.

After being returned to street patrol, Rodney was assigned by his lieutenant to the 3pm to 11pm shift back in Georgetown, where he had worked for six years before becoming the Captain's driver. Immediately after the kidnapping all shifts were changed to 12 hours.

The Second District covers Georgetown and much of the city's northwest quadrant: Foggy Bottom, Palisades, Spring Valley, Glover Park, *et al*, meaning mostly rich and mostly white people. It is a generally low crime area compared to some other D.C. districts and safer and more pleasant for police work.

Georgetown residents have purposefully kept the Metro from building a station in the neighborhood, the never admitted reason being to keep young black teenagers, who might use the subway system to get there, out of the stores and off the sidewalks, thereby, at least in the minds of Georgetowners, reducing crime.

Rodney B. Williams is known by the other cops at the Second Precinct station house as "B-Rod" because of his middle initial and the fact that he is the opposite of A-Rod, a New York Yankees third baseman and steroid-taking womanizer.

B-Rod is a homebody and family man. His sweet wife had died from the complications of childbirth five years before, leaving him with a baby girl and her 3-year old sister to care for. His elderly mother, Stella, moved right in from her nearby apartment to his small house a few blocks away on 5th Street, Southeast.

Stella Williams is cheery and industrious and the biggest influence in Rodney's life. He loves her dearly. She had given him the middle name Byron, after the English poet, an awkward fact he keeps out of the stationhouse, telling everyone who ever asks that his middle initial stood for "Bob".

Stella packs his daily lunch, his "snack pack," in a faded tin lunch box with smiling giraffes on it – she had bought it for Rodney at the National Zoo when he was 12. From its spacious interior he now extracts two of his mother's tasty homemade doughnuts with crispy bacon bits pressed into the real Pennsylvania Dutch maple syrup glaze.

"Oooh, whoa, good," says B-Rod aloud, as he sinks his teeth into the morning confection and eyeballs the news crews and gawkers gathered at the mouth of N Street.

B-Rod is a good father and a good son. He is also a good cop, at least in the sense that he is honest and reliable, if not a ball of fire. His police academy class was a human train wreck.

In 1989, the crack-smoking D.C. mayor Marion Barry ("the bitch set me up") had been responsible for setting low recruitment standards in replenishing the large numbers of retiring uniformed officers, most of whom were white.

About 1500 new police cadets were accepted at the police academy under Barry's confused affirmative action plan, and pressure from Congress. Some could barely read or write, many had lengthy felony records but most were graduated from the academy anyway, given a gun and awesome personal power.

The city's police lunacy is still talked about in national law enforcement circles. It was finally reported by the Washington Post on its front page in August of 1994, years after it had begun.

WaPo is not always a reliable chronicler of negative stories about local D.C. government. It has covered up a great deal. The paper does not like criticizing the African-

114

American leadership. WaPo was an early and ardent supporter of Marion Barry, the emerging politician, back when he wore a multicolored African dashiki, pretended he was an American-born Jomo Kenyatta and was given to crazy, radical statements.

There were men and women in B-Rods' class, overweight, unable to do even one chin-up, people who never learned how to handcuff a suspect or even how the cuffs worked. One officer appeared in court to testify at a jury trial wearing baggy shorts, hanging low in the back, a T-shirt, untied tennis shoes, and a half-dozen gold chains.

Other officers refused to remove their designer sunglasses on the witness stand. More than 200 members of the class of 1989-90 were arrested for murder, robbery, rape theft, perjury and other crimes. The Metropolitan Police were known as the Blue Circus.

More than 100 officers were not allowed to make arrests. They couldn't write a sufficiently intelligible report for court. They were given meaningless jobs.

By 1994, Washington, D.C., was being called the "Murder Capital of America." Many people were afraid to leave their homes in some mostly black neighborhoods, or to use public transportation.

Some of the new police officers belonged to the "R Street Crew" led by the infamous crack dealer Rayful Edmonds, who employed his mother and 150 other black Washingtonians. They were selling 2,000 kilos of cocaine a week to street dealers.

The gang murdered more than 400 people in two years and attempted to kill a local pastor, Reverend Bynum, who had the courage to lead an anti-drug, anti-R Street Crew march through his Orleans Place neighborhood. The minister barely survived after being shot 12 times with various handguns.

An example of this municipal lunacy was finally reported by the Washington Post, but not until 1994. The first paragraph in the front-page story grabbed the reader's attention:

> *"Two ambitions drove Charles Smith in the summer of 1989. The first was to up his income as a member of the R Street Crew, a murderous drug gang. The second was to join the police force. By fall, Smith had achieved both."*

Smith was in a Prince George's County jail when he received the letter accepting him to the Washington Metropolitan Police Academy. Smith lasted about a year after graduation. He was still selling PCP but was caught and fired from the PD.

Ultimately the Washington, D.C., U.S. Attorney's Office, then led by Eric Holder, later to become Obama's Attorney General, kept the list of 185 sworn and armed Metropolitan police officers who were too incompetent to write a report or appear in court. A couple of them, swore a former police officer under oath, were borderline retarded. None of them were allowed to make an arrest, though none of them were ever fired, either.

Eric Holder never made any serious attempt to have the egregious situation corrected. The public and the judiciary were unaware of any of this until a conservative magazine with a national readership published a piece by a young staff writer who reported the shocking facts about the dangerous disintegration of the police department. This became a widely circulated story. An informal network of federal judges passed it from judicial chamber to judicial chamber. The facts were so shocking it pushed a reluctant Washington Post into finally investigating the outrageous results of the affirmative action hiring of minority police cadets by the city in 1989-90, four years after the damage had been done.

Chapter Nineteen

The N Street area in the Georgetown neighborhood is generally subdued and quiet. Now it is being picked apart with the finest of media toothcombs.

Glamorous TV personalities like Diane Sawyer, Nora O'Donnell and Satchel Ronan Farrow are seen on its sidewalks. Recently, through DNA lifted from the rim of his teacup by an enterprising UK Daily Mail reporter, Farrow had proven *not* to be the son of Frank Sinatra as his mother Mia had publicly suggested years after Sinatra's death. Ronan's mother was unavailable for media comment. Wearing colorful tribal garb, Mia Farrow was in Eritrea attempting to adopt an entire Hausa family of 17 from a remote village.

Celebrity journalists are joined by news teams from AP, the Washington Post, the New York Times, the New York Post and others who are spread through the neighborhood collecting vignettes and info for stories, pictures, maps and diagrams depicting the names and history of N Street.

These are all sidebars, as there is no real news to be had. The kidnappers and Hillary have disappeared and have left no clues in their wake.

Katie Couric, her daytime talk show dead and buried, does a TV standup for Yahoo News in the middle of 31st and N Street, which has been blocked by police from

Wisconsin all the way to 28th. Yellow police tape and more than a thousand gawkers are spread at the intersections.

"This big gray house behind me is where, last night at 7pm, during a fancy fundraiser for her presidential campaign, Hillary Clinton was kidnapped. This is the side gate from which she was hustled by two phony Secret Service agents into a waiting SUV - a black vehicle designed to look like one of Mrs. Clinton's security cars. They call them 'War Wagons' in Washington. It was sitting in this driveway, at the side of 3051 N Street, in the bosom of Washington's fashionable Georgetown." She turns and points, "Up there at the end of the street is Martin's Tavern where JFK proposed to Jackie O in a booth, next to another booth, where years before, the State Department's Alger Hiss accepted an expensive Oriental rug from his Soviet Spy Handler. Amazing neighborhood."– Katie Couric, Yahoo News

"The World War II war correspondent Ernie Pyle lived on the top floor at 3051 N in rooms he rented from the society woman who then owned the house. From his front window, across the Georgetown rooftops, Pyle wrote in 1943, a few weeks before he left for the Pacific and was killed on an island near Okinawa by Japanese machine gun fire, that he could see American P38 fighter planes flying over the Potomac River." – Neil Cavuto, Fox Business Channel

"The house is not flashy, but it is very large and one with many rich neighbors, past and present. It was a hospital during the Civil War, and President Lincoln visited wounded soldiers here. Senator John Sherman Cooper, no relation to me, lived in that house over there for fifty years and with his wife Lorraine was very socially prominent. My mother knew them both." – Anderson Cooper, CNN

"The house here at 3051 N Street is five floors, about 20 rooms and a dozen fire places. A neighbor says the finished basement has a large living room with a billiard table and player piano, a walk in vault, and a swimming pool and sauna, put in by an owner in the 1970's.". with a trompe l'oeil painting that covers a complete wall. It is of Gibraltar in the Iberian Peninsula as seen from a terrace at Malcom Forbes' house in Tangier. Forbes was a friend of that owner". – Brett Baier, Special Report, Fox News

"None of the N Street neighbors, the rich and famous, among those still living, is seen as a serious suspect in the crime itself or in its aftermath, although people from the party and neighborhood are still being questioned." – Larry King, CNN, who was having dinner in a back booth at The Palm Restaurant with his wife's younger sister Shannon when he heard about the snatch. He called Jeff Zucker at CNN and volunteered to tape a field piece.

"Pamela Harriman, doyenne of the Clinton Democrats, lived in her husband Averell's old house at 3058 N. Street. Pam's lover in her later years, J. Carter Brown, head of the

120

National Gallery, lived in the house directly behind 3051 N Street, next to the author Kitty Kelley. He could be seen occasionally trotting home from Pam Harriman's by early-rising neighbors, once in a bathrobe, his WASPy hair tousled by sleep. The general belief that Brown was gay seems unfounded, not that there is anything wrong with that." – Rachel Maddow, MSNBC-TV

"A couple of doors down from Pamela Harriman's is the former home of Abraham Lincoln's son Robert Todd Lincoln, head of the Pullman Railroad Car Company. The enormous house was owned by the Washington Post's Ben Bradlee, now gone, and his third wife, the shrewish, social climbing Sally Quinn." - Nancy Grace, who had once been attacked by Quinn in a Post Style piece.

"John Kennedy, when he was president, would occasionally have sex and smoke a little dope in the Bradlee's guesthouse with Bradlee's sister-in-law Mary Meyer, the wife of CIA official Cord Meyer. Mary was shot to death alongside the Georgetown Canal, a few blocks away, less than a year after Kennedy died. Her murder was never solved. Her diary was seized from Bradlee by James Angleton, the CIA counter intelligence chief." – Chris Plante, WMAL Radio

"Jackie Kennedy owned 3075 N, bought with the help of Averell Harriman a few weeks after the assassination in 1963. Mrs. Kennedy's N Street house was later sold to Yolande Fox, a former Miss America and the widow of the robber-baron capitalist Charles Fox, who founded 20th Century Fox studios, thereby being singly responsible, at least early on, for the ultimate creation of the Fox News Channel." – Megyn Kelly, the Kelly File, Fox News

"The Virginia-born journalist Brit Hume lived with his wife Kim on the other side of the Harriman houses, directly across from 3051. One Harriman house was used as an office, often by the famously insecure diplomat Dick Holbrooke, whose sucking up to Mrs. Harriman seemed boundless." – Richard Johnson, New York Post

"The last house on the block, on the corner of N and 30th, diagonally across from that of the late Ben Bradlee, was the home of former Attorney General John Mitchell, who lived there with his lover Mrs. Mary Benton Gore Dean - the owner of the Fairfax Hotel and second cousin of Al Gore - until he collapsed and died of a heart attack in front of the home one November afternoon in 1988. Some called it sidewalk justice!" - Bob Woodward, Washington Post

Chapter Twenty

Lieutenant Gus Bruneman, Tactical Squad Commander of the Montgomery County Sheriff's Office, is feeling jumpy. He is out on a loading dock at the Rockville substation with all this work to do, interesting work, and he is now being called away.

Bruneman had been planning to spend his morning sorting through the latest load of equipment dumped on the sheriff's department by the Feds via a grant process from the Department of Defense and its "1033" Excess Property Transfer Program for state and local law enforcement agencies. The program had expanded significantly during the Obama Administration and was now handing out $700 million a year in "used" property although much of it was actually brand new and had never been used at all.

"Just amazing excess, completely loony," thinks Gus, an ex-Marine. "But big time fun!" It was like being back in the 2nd Force Recon Company at Camp Lejeune, North Carolina, with more than enough goodies to start a frigging war of your own.

Gus himself had filled out a one-page DoD order form for another armored vehicle last year - the Sheriff's Office now had six - that stated "INDICATE YOUR PREFERENCE FOR A VEHICLE THAT HAS EITHER WHEELS OR TRACKS LIKE A TANK. (Check a box). DELIVERY

WILL BE MADE IN 14 DAYS. Gus had checked WHEELS, but the imagined sound of tank tracks clanking down Wisconsin Avenue in Bethesda, Maryland, had considerable appeal.

Gus chortles to himself thinking about the chief of the tiny town of Keene, New Hampshire, who, when asked by the media how he justified taking a brand new tactical armored vehicle from DoD, said with enthusiasm, "Hey! They offered it and we can use it to patrol main street at our yearly Pumpkin Festival."

"The dude really said that. These are crazy times," thinks Gus.

The 1033 Program has its roots in the old War on Drugs, the idea being that if local law enforcement people were going to fight such a war then, shit, they should look like warriors, not cops.

Almost a million dollars in new tactical gear, all war fighting military equipment, had arrived, including 27 M4 assault rifles, field medical packs, hundreds of wool blankets, a dozen 9mm pistols, two cammo-painted trucks, 3 grenade launchers, four crates of gas masks, 100 cases of MRE's, two dozen night-vision goggles, 25 two person tents, four shoulder-fired armor-piercing rockets, a slew of new radio controlled flash-bang grenades capable of being rolled on tiny wheels to a door or wall and detonated, blowing the living shit out of everything for a dozen feet, and two bomb-disposing robots.

Four new battering rams with titanium heads and cases of 5.56mm ammo for the M4 automatic rifles are stacked on the back loading dock of the Sheriff's Office. A dozen beanbag firing Benelli M4 shotguns are in a locked wooden case.

A second fully armored GNQ 25 vehicle is now parked in the TAC squad space outside. GNQ stands for Give No Quarter, and it surely didn't. It had arrived, brand new via long distance hauler from the factory outside Lexington, Kentucky, a week ago. It bristles with complicated communications gear and radar components.

"The old Sheriff's Office is beginning to look like Seal Team Six's weapons depot with all these remarkable toys," thinks Bruneman.

Now this - he has gotten a call from Captain Skiles, Ruthie Skiles, his supervisor, ordering him to take her place at a law enforcement conference that very day in a Baltimore hotel. He has to be there for lunch in two hours, and he is going to be stuck there into the early evening.

"What annoying bullshit," he thinks. She didn't even apologize for the no warning notice. She just said she couldn't make it and he should represent the Sheriff's

Office, be nice to the Sheriff himself, Binky Collins, who would be there, too, and say hello to the Governor for her.

"Weird that she cancelled," he thinks, because former Governor Martin O'Malley of Maryland, the handsome crackpot egotist whom Ruthie loves, is going to speak about the problems facing released prisoners. This on behalf of some goofy group called Inmates for Justice. The irony, thinks Bruneman, is that the prisoners in the huge Baltimore City Jail were actually running the place with the aid of female guards, of which half, at any given time, were pregnant by prisoners, some for the second or third time. MOM (the derisive acronym for Martin O'Malley) knew about the jail conditions and corruption and did nothing. MOM has been basically unemployed since his Lt Governor Anthony Brown went down to crushing defeat in the 2014 election to an obscure Republican businessman named Larry Hogan, who replaced MOM and his wasteful, arrogant tax & spend policies.

O'Malley is the very favorite politician of Ruthie Skies. "So, this conference would be right up her Democratic Party alley, right up her affirmative action, feminist butt," he thinks. "Why would she want to miss it? I wonder what's going on."

Gus pulls loose one of the crates of MRE's. It has "Meals Ready to Eat - 1300 calories each per unit" stenciled on the sides. He pulls out one of the packs and looks at it.

126

"These things are actually pretty good," he thinks. "Nothing like the miserable C-Rats we used to get. Course in the old days they always had a small four-pack of butts in them. Lucky Strikes or Chesterfields." He smiles with the remembrance.

"Smoking lamp is lit. Light 'em if you got 'em," barked the Gunny. Somewhere along the wussified way, Headquarters Marine Corps had blown the old smoking lamp into smithereens!

The plastic MRE bag lists its menu: spaghetti with meat sauce, bread and cheese spread, a small bottle of Tabasco sauce, Skittles, Chiclets, dried cranberries, and pretzels.

"Skittles? I guess that's to replace the unfiltered cigarettes," thinks Gus. "Well," he mumbles to himself, taking one of the packs in his fist, "I may have a picnic in the car on the way to Baltimore 'cause I'm going to be late for that friggin' governor's lunch."

Chapter Twenty One

Lt. Clam Box Kelly hits the Tarry Awhile home at 10am. Visiting hours are on and people are in and out. No one pays any attention to him, as he perambulates up and down the halls past dozens of after breakfast patients in bathrobes, snoozing in their wheelchairs or just staring into space.

The only staffer there who actually knows him by sight is Miss Hamburger and she wouldn't be on duty until 3, she had said in her text. He finds the room with Mildred Paperman. The door is open.

She is asleep and he scurries in, holding a printout of Miss Hamburger's photo and the BOLO circular of the Hillary kidnapping, also with her photo, in each hand.

He bends over Mildred and then squeezes her arm. "Hello dear, just checking to see how you are feeling today," he says unctuously, as she opens her eyes briefly.

"Ah, they are gray blue," he thinks. "That would be right. About 5'7, maybe 150 pounds. Small double chin, heavy wrinkles around her eyes, slightly rabbity front teeth."

He pulls up the sheet six inches from the bottom and looks at her legs. Fat ankles ("kankles" they used to call them in high school. Dairymaid's legs.) That's why she always wore pants. He glances from photo to photo. "My God! It is her!" he thinks to himself.

He wakes her again. "You are Hillary, yes?" he asks in a low soothing voice. Mildred can hear him, but barely. She thinks he said, "You are Millie, yes?" She nods, and returns to snoring.

A thin, elderly man with a bad comb-over is watching from the room across the way. He is perched on a motorized wheelchair. Clam Box stops and says hello to the old fellow. There are two other men in the suite, both in similar electric wheel chairs, one with oxygen in a nasal tube clamped on his nose; both are following him with their eyes.

"I just stopped in to see my aunt," says Kelly. "She's not doing so well, so I'll be back later today."

The man at the door is reading a New York Post. His name, according to the tape on his wheelchair is Ken Corrigan. Next to his name is a Redskins decal with the profile of a warrior in headdress. Mr. Corrigan has a nose like that Indian chief, notes Clam Box.

"So how are you, Mr. Corrigan?" Kelly asks. All three men reply with grunts and mumbles.

"We are brothers, if you are wondering," says Ken, the man closest to the door. Clam Box notices that the three have a strong familial resemblance, prominent noses, and high foreheads. "Triplets?" asks Clam Box.

"They are twins, Leonard and Dennis," says Ken. "I am two years older. I'm 86." Ken folds his paper in his lap. "We are Ken and Len and Den Corrigan, known as the Right-Way Corrigans. Our uncle Doug was 'Wrong Way Corrigan.' He flew non-stop to Ireland from New York in 1938. He was trying to fly to California but his compass didn't work right."

Ancient history of which Clam Box is vaguely aware.

"Well, that is great," says Clam Box, at a loss for words. "Nice that you three are together," he mutters uncomfortably.

"My brothers were born in November, 1932, a few days after FDR beat Hoover and brought the country down the road to socialism and now to the fascism that we have with this Obama crowd, the government trouncing on people's rights and taking all their money in taxes."

"Oh, right," says Kelly, not wanting to get into a political argument, particularly on a subject about which he knows next to nothing. "Hey, have you seen anybody visiting my aunt?" He points across the hall to Miss Paperman's room.

"One man," says a brother from across the room, with the oxygen tubes in his nose. "I'm Len. Her only visitor is an old guy in a very bad wig and sunglasses. A disguise. He sits and mutters to her but she doesn't seem to say anything back. He's probably hiding from the IRS or some such."

"OK," says Clam Box. "I'd better push off. But, I shall return. You men have a nice day."

Clam Box gives a half-assed cop salute. "By the by," he says, "Were you three in a business together, uh, back in the old days?"

"Yes. We were debt collectors for the government Mafia - strong arm men out to enforce the rules on paying vigorish, called taxes by the bureaucrats." says Ken. The trio chortle in a brotherly way, honking through their great noses.

"Just kidding," says the brother with the oxygen clip. "We had an accounting firm for more than 50 years, Corrigan, Corrigan and Corrigan, in downtown Washington."

"Those are pretty nifty wheel chairs you have got here," says Clam Box. "They must have cost an arm and a leg." Clam Box mugs a mock wince. "Ouch! Sorry for the bad choice of words."

"No offense," says Ken.

"They were free," says one of the other brothers. "It's a big fraud. Everyone in this place has one whether they need it or not. Half of them don't. We keep a dozen on the back porch and use them for hallway races on the second Friday of the month. Come on by sometime. We take bets. We call it Geriatric Bumper Car Night because a few of the drivers never remember what they are doing, so there is an occasional pile-up."

"We've got one scooter with a big beer cooler tied to the seat. We fill it with ice and bottles of cheap beer. We sell 'em for 50 cents each."

"These little puppies are part of a big Medicare scam," says one of the twins, tapping the chair with a long yellow fingernail. "The Scooter Store out in Texas makes them for around $800 apiece then they charge the federal government $5,000. They advertise them as free on TV. The doctor here just writes a prescription for each new patient and they get a scooter, whether they need it or not, courtesy of the taxpayer. I figure the doctor and Tarry Awhile get paid off by the manufacturer."

"The lucrative Medicare scams used to be in the shoe-insert biz - $500 for custom made orthotics, or orthopedic braces or electric Nerve Stimulation Kits or prosthetic legs. They spent millions on people who had both of their original two legs."

"Since 1999," says Ken, "the morons who run Medicare have spent more than $9 billion in tax money for about 3 million scooters and motorized wheel chairs. And they have no idea how many people really need them."

132

"Yeah, well," huffs Don into his nasal oxygen tubes, "we do have a lot of fun with them."

Clam Box's head is reeling with all of this information. "If I ever do get to run the FBI or the State Police I will make serious inquiry into this bullshit fraud," he thinks. "Meanwhile, I have some clams to fry and I can practically smell them cracking in the hot oil."

"Gentlemen," he beams. "It's been great talking with you. I'll come back for the wheelchair races some night," he says as he heads down the hall to the front door. He calls out over his shoulder; "I may even see you sooner than that!"

Clam Box is in and out of that nursing home in less than 15 minutes - just like a Mexican bordello, as his father used to say.

Chapter Twenty Two

Back in his car, Clam Box has to hold tight to the steering wheel as the incredible ramifications of this discovery race through his brain.

His hands are trembling, as he thinks of the likely TV movie, starring a very cool Clam Box look-alike. It might even be a real movie, like in theatres.

He tries to think of an actor who could play his part, someone tough and masculine but nice looking and good with the ladies, too. "Nicholas Cage maybe, though, come to think of it, he isn't all that good looking and he has that weak chin, like a receding tide of flesh. In fact, he looks like a white Eric Holder in the chin department, and he also looks suspiciously short," Clam Box thinks. Half those fucking guys stand on a box when they are making movies. Someone had once told Clam Box about the apparently diminutive Paul Newman. "Bruce Willis might work or, hey, one of the Wahlberg brothers." He can't remember their first names. "Oh, man this is so excellent."

He calls Ruthie, who is waiting nervously in her office trying to absorb a manual about Police Special Weapons and Tactics as quickly as she can after sending Lt. Gus Bruneman off on a wild goose hunt to Baltimore.

Like Clam Box, she has been swimming in thoughts of glory and accolades since he called her with the rundown from his informant at eight this morning, and explained his plan to personally verify the identity of the "subject" they had begun calling Hillary.

"It is *her*. Not a doubt in my frigging pea-brain," says Clam Box, who tells himself to watch his language, as Ruthie doesn't like swearing or the typical cop crudities.

"I put my face in her face and got her to admit it. It *is* Hillary. She even said so. She is drugged and restrained. I see no threat whatsoever to her security. If they were going to hurt her they would have done it already. And I didn't see any security force that could pose a threat to us. No guards at all. They are using drugs to keep her quiet and out of it."

"This is fantastic," says Ruthie, silently grateful for the positive news, as she is intimidated, even a little frightened, by the idea of leading a SWAT team on a raid on anything, much less a crowded nursing home.

Ruthie is suddenly seized by a spasm of intense curiosity. "Who are the kidnappers?" she says. "Why are they doing this? What do you think they want?" She directs these queries to Clam Box.

"Captain," he says, "I have no clue. But one thing I do know. We are about to rescue Hillary Clinton. You and me."

"Room 35 at the nursing home," says Clam Box. "My confidential informant, her name is Hamburger, she's coming in early, about 2pm. She said the kidnapper, the guy in the wig and shades, comes in around 3. We should plan the raid, led by you and me, for four o'clock, grab the kidnapper and liberate Hillary at the same moment."

"We'll let the Feds deal with the nursing home owner, who is clearly in on this, but lives in Florida, after we get the former first lady to safety," adds Clam Box.

"Sacre bleu, c'est tres encroyable," says Ruthie in the thin French accent she sometimes employs for exclamatory effect.

What an ass-bite this woman is, thinks Clam Box, whose voice is nonetheless smiling on the phone. He is deliriously happy. How can he not be, poised as he is on the brink of international fame and a lifetime of on-going public gratitude and adoring credit? ("See that old fellow? That's Peter "Clam Box" Kelly, retired FBI director, the man who saved Hillary Clinton's life - a man with real moxie!") He can hear it now, even if those kudos have to be shared with this female dickwad.

"You got any favorite TV types you want to tip to the action, Ruthie? Just one would do it - their video will go around the world within an hour. No sense in cluttering the sidewalk in front of the Tarry Awhile with media creeps. Reach out to someone you know and you can make that reporter grateful for life."

"I've got just the ticket," says Ruthie, thinking of a good-looking local woman reporter, Tessa Jones, at the ABC affiliate in Washington. Ruthie had met Tessa at a party recently and she had received a definite vibe from her when she was introduced as a sheriff's captain.

Ruthie was wearing civvies at the time. In fact, it was her huggy little cream-colored St. John knit, with the hem that rose almost to her muff. She had seen admiration, and maybe, we can hope can't we, she thinks, desire in Tessa's eyes as she looked her over.

"Yes," she thinks, "I would definitely like to pull little Tessa's thong off with my teeth."

"I'll get her over here and we'll lock her and her cameraman in my office until we are ready to mount-up and ride out," Ruthie says with a grin into the phone. "Mount up!" she giggles to herself with thoughts of the tasty Tessa, "No pun intended."

Ruthie and Clam Box wait in his office until the text comes in from Clam Box's informant, Miss Hamburger, shortly after 3. It says that the man in the wig has just arrived and is headed to the subject's room.

The pair then swing into feverish action, planning to claim later that the tip came so quickly, without warning, and that they had to act with such compelling immediacy, there was no time to try and track down the sheriff or SWAT team commander Lt. Bruneman, who are both away in a Baltimore hotel.

Ruthie orders a dozen SWAT team members, who are playing dominoes or lifting weights in their substation squad room, to be geared-up and ready with both heavy vehicles in 30 minutes. The target for this operation is two miles away. They will receive details on the scene right before the action. The operation is highly classified.

Ruthie and Clam Box have their gear laid out in the office on a table and then help each other into it: black canvas overalls, knee and elbow pads, front and back Kevlar bullet proof vests that snap together, black helmets with a smoky visor, a gas mask, a first aid kit, a tear gas canister, a pepper spray canister, a Taser gun, and two stun grenades ("flash bangs") all hanging from hooks on the front and side. There is a Glock pistol and heavy belt with 20 rounds of ammo, an M4 carbine with a carry sling and 50 rounds of hollow point ammo on a bandolier, and a pair of black canvas and leather gloves. There is even a military canteen, filled with water, for first aid in washing pepper spray from suffering eyes.

Clam Box, who is wearing his regular high top leather police shoes, is finished.

Ruthie is almost dressed but needs assistance with the heavy Kevlar vests, which Clam Box gives her, working the snaps into place. She has forgotten about boots and is wearing medium high heels with black straps. The trousers are thankfully a little long and almost cover her feet, though her painted toes, which match the dark red color of her nails, flash through a bit as she walks.

She looks at her nails and then the gloves. "No way am I wearing those gloves," she says, mindful of paying $25 to have her nails done by that cute Vietnamese girl down on Berry Avenue two days ago. Gloves like these would destroy her nails.

She slings her carbine over her shoulder. She is having trouble walking with all this gear, and in heels yet. "Please Lord, don't make me have to run," she prays.

Tessa Jones and her cameraman, a wiry fellow named Stanley Mace, but called Ace, are in the outer office waiting. They have not yet been told what the story is, just that it will be the news event of their lives, never to be duplicated.

Ruthie rates a driver, a young female deputy she hand picked. Ruthie and Clam Box and Tessa squeeze into the back of the gray unmarked Ford, Ace Mace sits in front.

They drive to the Rite-Aid pharmacy parking lot, a block from the Tarry Awhile Nursing home, to meet with the 12-man team that has quickly assembled and are ready to load back in to the two massive assault vehicles, now sitting parked next to each other, rumbling ominously, like hungry prehistoric carnivores.

When Ruthie put her lips near Tessa Jones' pretty small ear to whisper that they have found Hillary Clinton and are about to rescue her, Tessa gasps, and reaches out and squeezes Ruthie's kneepad, hard. She whispers, "Oh my fucking word!"

Tessa leans forward and says, "Ace, hold your hat. I'll tell you what we are going to be shooting when we get out of the car. Captain Skiles just told me. You are not going to believe this."

Chapter Twenty-Three

Police vehicles block off both ends of the street that fronts the nursing home, a one story wooden building with a screened porch in front and on one side. There are about 60 patients, many of them permanent, and a dozen staffers on the day shift.

The inside of Tarry Awhile is laid out as a T, with patients' rooms at the end of the main corridor and more rooms on both the right and left hand sides of the hall. The "subject" is in the last room on the right-hand hallway, on the left – the back corner, far out of the way.

The street is sealed with a marked sheriff's car at either end. A city ambulance and four EMT's, completely in the dark as to why they are there, have assembled in front of the building. Ace Mace and Tessa Jones and their video camera are in position on the walkway by the front door. One large armored vehicle lumbers up the alley to the right of the building, with four men to cover the rear.

The other GNQ 25 drives up on the sidewalk, and six troopers in full SWAT regalia including assault rifles, one man carrying a ballistic shield, another a battering ram, led by Clam Box and Ruthie, leap out and bound up the walk.

Ace captures this on video, opening with a shot of Tessa in the foreground, holding a mike and looking down the walk as the vehicle doors open and disgorge the team. Clam

Box and Ruthie are in front, sweating and huffing and puffing, but no one can tell through the helmets and coveralls. The moment is dramatic.

A few neighbors are out on the sidewalks but are being kept back behind yellow tape by uniformed sheriff's deputies. Nursing home staffers are frozen in place inside, some of them backed against the main corridor wall, confused by the approaching, unknown police action.

Miss Hamburger stands holding a clipboard, already feeling part of history. "Right this way," she says to Clam Box, whose eyes she recognizes through the smoky helmet shield, and she moves smartly down the hall to Mildred Paperman's room.

Bernard Kovacs has been reading the Wall Street Journal next to Mildred's bed. She is asleep. He half rises from his chair when he hears what sounds like an approaching crowd of people.

Miss Hamburger flies into the room, followed by Ruthie and Clam Box, like two screaming Valkyries, Bernard thinks. They look like people dressed in crow costumes. The larger of them lands on him and knocks him to the linoleum floor as the pair shouts, "Get down, get down, don't resist." Clam Box shouts, "Stop resisting or I'll Taser you, shit bird!"

Barnard isn't resisting but Clam Box has his knee in his back and the pressure is flattening his colostomy bag, now under his right hip, and he is trying to position himself to preserve his dignity. Clam Box is holding the Taser gun and it fires by accident, sending the wired dart right up the starched skirt of Miss Hamburger, who is standing over Bernard trying to help subdue him by striking him in the head with her clipboard.

The Taser dart plunges into the soft underside of her lower abdomen and she crashes to the floor, twitching terribly and knocking Ruthie's feet out from under her.

Ruthie goes down with her finger on the trigger of the M4 assault carbine and it fires a burst of eight hollow point bullets, four of which strike Clam Box on his back and right side, flattening with terrific impact and pain against the Kevlar, but not piercing it. One bullet knocks a flash-bang grenade off Clam Box's belt to the floor where it explodes, temporarily blinding and deafening Ruthie, who has landed on her butt, but is now flat out and unconscious, lying in a heap with Miss Hamburger, also blinded and deafened and still twitching, and Clam Box, who isn't moving at all. Bernard Kovacs is at the bottom of the pile.

Another bullet strikes the large steel oxygen tank in the corner of the Corrigan brothers' room and it explodes, rising like a NASA rocket through the ceiling, and then the roof, landing on and severely damaging the hood of a new green Prius parked at the curb outside, near the ambulance, whose EMT's, leaning on their vehicle listening to the shooting and explosions inside with considerable added wonder, watch it emerge like a missile from the nursing home and then return to earth twenty feet from them.

The roof is now on fire, fed by a carton of 1000 Depends diapers in the closet next to the Corrigans' room, and fire truck sirens can be heard just a few blocks away.

Ace Mace and Tessa Jones, having captured all of the events inside, race out to film the arrival of the fire trucks and another county ambulance which has been sent in response to dozens of 911 calls about the explosions at Tarry Awhile. They then turn run back inside and down the hall to the pile of seemingly dead bodies.

Inside, watching the attack on the poor old fellow visiting Miss Paperman from their room, and now watching what appears to be an escalation to full warfare, the three Corrigan brothers are in their wheel chairs. They have donned metal bedpans as helmets. Ken, Den and Len are lined up like charioteers.

Moaning comes from under the pile of bodies. Ken rolls his chair over to Miss Hamburger, who is on her back, the Taser wire running up under her uniform's skirt. Ken reaches down, puts his hand up her dress, closes his eyes out of modesty, and delicately extracts the dart from the dimpled folds of her tummy.

144

Ken leans over and pulls at Bernard Kovacs' sport coat - he is the source of the moans - and drags him further into the room. Ken reaches down and pulls the keys off a ring he notices on Clam Box's vest. He examines the keys, finds the simplest, hands them to Len who has rolled in, holding his bedpan helmet on his head with his hand. Len fiddles with the keys for moment, figures them out, and releases Bernie from his handcuffs.

Ruthie is dazed and seeing double but she has watched all this through heavy lids. "Wait," she shouts at Ken and Len. "That man is a suspect in a kidnapping. Leave those cuffs on him. Stop that right now."

She struggles to her feet and leans against the doorjamb. She points to Mildred, wheezing and asleep in the bed, and says, "That is Hillary Clinton right there! The former First Lady! We are rescuing her! Desist, immediately!" She reaches for her Glock but everything has shifted. She can't find it on her hip and pulls out a canvas wrapped canteen in error.

The third Corrigan brother rolls up and listens. He looks down and sees Ruthie's painted toes and high heels. He all along has assumed she was a man but now he also sees the painted nails on the hand pointing the canteen.

"By God, she is a *tranny,* probably from the damned IRS," he shouts and runs his wheelchair into the back of Ruthie's legs, catapulting her into the wall, where she is knocked unconscious, the canteen in her hand slowly gurgling water over the unconscious form of Lt. Peter "Clam Box" Kelly, whose dreams of heading the Maryland State Police or the FBI are likely gone forever.

Ace Mace and an incredulous Tessa Jones are videotaping all of this. Ace then tilts from the now unconscious Ruthie, after shooting a close-up of her Jimmy Choo shoes and painted toes, pans to the still unconscious Clam Box, to the delirious, sobbing Miss Hamburger, who is sitting against the bed, to Barnard Kovacs who is massaging his wrists and trying to stand, to the three Corrigan brothers in their shiny steel helmets (a photo of which makes the next day's New York Post front page with a headline that says, "Right Way Corrigan Boys Battle Police over Phony Hillary —and Win") to a great shot of the firemen and EMT's jogging up the hall pushing gurneys before them.

The entire TV film, edited, runs almost twelve minutes and is broadcast around the world, in every country, within two hours of Ace and Tessa getting it back to their newsroom in Washington.

Hillary Clinton is still missing, not a whit closer to being found, but even a meaningless TV depiction, if it is graphic, dramatic and interesting - and this was all three - is an audience grabber. It is seen by an estimated 460 million people, the largest audience in the history of television.

146

Chapter Twenty-Four

At the rented safe house on Dent Place, Hillary is locked in the small bedroom. It's the third day she's been here. One and Two have been leaving her alone. She can lift the desk and pull off the leg. "A weapon if I need it," she thinks to herself. Everyone who knows her knows she's not someone to be fucked with. Given half a chance she'd use it. But for now, she'll bide her time and figure out what's going on.

The bedroom door is bolted from the outside so she has stopped trying to force it open. Instead she focuses on the room and its contents.

The walls are painted a pleasant yellow. No windows, no curtains. A simple wooden bed and a headboard, even a reading lamp attached, with floral sheets and a bedspread that looks clean. She lifts up the mattress to check beneath. Nothing there.

There's no heater along the floor or heat duct in the walls or ceiling. She surmises that the heat must come in from the main room. The furnace is on the other side of the basement. The temperature is comfortable.

The dresser and desk are old pieces of solid wood furniture. Perhaps 40 years old. No IKEA magic here, although she wouldn't actually know an IKEA piece if she saw it.   Ethan Allen, perhaps, the Kellogg Collection maybe, but not IKEA.

She goes through the dresser drawers. They yield nothing, but when she pulls one of the drawers of the old desk out completely she finds what appears to be a water bill dated October, 1981, stuffed in the back. There's an address on it - 3237 Dent Place! A pang of relief trembles down her body. "I know where I am. This desk has been here forever. This must be the address," she thinks to herself. "Now I just need to let someone know." She muses over this. The "someone" for whom she has a mailing address would surely help.

As she starts scheming on how to get a message to him, she paces the floor and then does some leg exercises. She normally loathes exercise.   But she feels minor league empowered and she wants to be fit enough to seize any physical opportunities that may present themselves.   She admired the physical prowess of the SEALS when they got bin-Laden, and she somehow envisions herself being heroic - rescuing herself, so to speak. She thinks back to Obama delaying his decision to go after bin-Laden and kill him, it seemed like forever. Part of it was that weakling Joe Biden. He didn't want to take the risk, even after Obama gave the go-ahead order, he whined and wussed against it to the end. Until it succeeded, that is, and then he couldn't stop talking about how cool it was.

Now one of the "boys" has turned a TV on in the outer room and she can hear some of the news.

"Turn the fucking volume up," she yells through the door. "At least let me hear what they're saying about me."

Wayne ponders it a bit and complies. He doesn't like to hear her cursing at him. He also feels a bit of compassion for her, as unhappy as a trapped possum.

"The news just says they're looking for you, Mrs. Clinton," he says through her door. "It says they have no clues where you are and no suspects. And it says your husband and daughter are worried."

Bill Clinton has been on every TV channel in the US and abroad, frequently tearing up, his shoulders heaving slightly, as he grieves for and reminisces at length about his beloved partner.

TV studio crews sometimes note that he seems to have a spring in his step, at least he does off camera – particularly as he flirts with and sometimes hits on various show bookers, production assistants and makeup women, but hey, everyone deals with grief differently, is the consensus.

Bill doesn't want Hillary hurt; he wants her to come home safe and healthy, just not too quickly. During the actual kidnapping Bill was in bed with a girlfriend at his large white Dutch Colonial house in the picturesque village of

Chappaqua, New York, 35 minutes by limousine from Manhattan.

His Friend with Benefits, he actually calls her that, is the pleasantly zaftig middle-aged wife of a rich garment manufacturer from the Bronx. She is an ardent Hillary supporter who has rationalized having sex with Hillary's husband as a patriotic act. Bill has encouraged this view. He is given to quoting Gennifer Flowers's book ("Passion and Betrayal" - 1995) in private with paramours. "Gennifer quotes me as saying that Hillary has gone down on more women than I ever have. Well, I did say that. 'Cause it is true. Now if you'll lay back, dear lady, I'm still tryin' to catch up with her."

Bill is wearing his maroon University of Arkansas Razorback sweatshirt and blue tighties, his favorite bedtime garb, as the pair rock and roll the night away, ignoring the ringing bedside telephone – until one of his security detail begins beating on the door, yelling, "Hillary has been kidnapped."

Bill wishes old Hill well in his private thoughts; they've been through a lot together over many years, but he is glad she is finally quiet for a while; not yelling at him or hectoring him or bothering him for constant political advice or bugging him as to where he has been and what or who he has been doing, always trying to trap him in inconsistencies, trying to catch him in what he calls fact-fudging.

150

"Did you send a text message to my husband yet?" Hillary asks.

"No, but we'll do it today," replies Wayne.

"What? You ass wipes, get it done. You said you would. He'll be worried."

"We'll do it, Ma'am. Today."

Chapter Twenty-Five

In the early afternoon of the fourth day of Hillary's captivity, Wayne sends Zipper out on his mission. He drives towards Woodbridge, Virginia, about 25 miles south of Washington, pulls off at the Route 123 exit just across the Occoquan River bridge, and heads over to the nearby McDonalds on Old Bridge Road.

He drives through the service line for a small cheeseburger and a caramel frappe. It's cold out, but the frappes are his favorite.

Leaving McDonalds, he heads across Old Bridge to the commuter parking lot, pulls in, parks, and gets the phone out.

He inserts the SIM card and turns on Hillary's iPhone. The home screen comes up, and he presses the messages icon. There is Bill's message, waiting to be sent. Zipper reads the message again to be sure it's what he remembers it to be, and he presses "send". Then he shuts off the phone and yanks the SIM card out. With no SIM card it can't be tracked. He pulls out of the commuter lot, goes east a few hundred yards, and turns south on I-95. His mission isn't over.

Less than a half-second after the text message is sent to Bill Clinton's phone, law enforcement is on it. Two FBI techs have been posted to AT&T, Hillary's carrier, to aid in tracking if her phone is used.

A tower near I-95 in Woodbridge is identified as the one that picked up and carried the message forward. The 'pings' and accompanying message last less than 10 seconds. If Hillary's phone is in Woodbridge, she may be there with it.

Law enforcement sinks its teeth right in. There is immediate excitement at the Find Hillary Task Force Headquarters in downtown Washington.

Meanwhile, Zipper is on his way out of Woodbridge. Thirty miles south of Fredericksburg, Virginia, he finds what he is looking for: The Flying J Truck Stop, a large service center crammed with diesel rigs, the drivers sleeping in their cabs or schmoozing in the restaurant. It's easy on, easy off for the interstate.

Pulling into the enormous parking lot, Zipper looks over the big trucks, many with their engines rumbling.

He watches a middle aged driver slide from the cab of a 16 wheeler hauling a 20-foot long Thermo King reefer van. On both sides of the truck is painted in red - "Frank Perdue Chicken - It Takes a Tough Man to Make a Tender Chicken." Zipper chuckles. "Hell," he thinks to himself. "It takes a tough man to kidnap a tender Hillary Clinton - not!"

Zipper continues to eye the driver as the man enters the main store. He's carrying a large insulated coffee mug that has Go Panthers printed on it. The truck engine is running.

Zipper slips the SIM card back into the phone but leaves it off. He gets out of his car and saunters over to the passenger side of the cab, an Isuzu Duramax, polished and shiny. Without attracting attention, he works his gloved hands around and inside one of the tire wells.

He duct-tapes Hillary's iPhone to the underside, covering it with tape but leaving the on-off switch uncovered.

Zipper waits on his haunches, leaning against a large wheel, peering through the undercarriage, until he sees the driver heading to the truck, swinging a plastic bag of doughnuts and sipping from his Skins mug. Zipper flicks on the phone. Perfect timing.

Within three minutes, the reefer van is rolling towards North Carolina. Zipper follows it out of the lot towards the interstate. As the driver heads south with Hillary's phone, Zipper turns north and heads back towards D.C. and Georgetown.

With a warning that her phone has been active, AT&T and law enforcement are on high alert for any further activation. Now cell towers north of Richmond, Virginia, are picking it up, tracking it as it makes its way south. Two helicopters from Fort Belvoir with tracking devices are quickly overhead, sorting the traffic below on I-95, and trying to identify from which vehicle the pings are coming. Two other helicopters filled with FBI SWAT members closely trail them, ready to pounce when the target vehicle is clearly ID'd.

On I-95, bopping along in his reefer van and listening to Hank Williams cranked up to full volume is Jimmy Akers, a likeable, good-natured Vietnam veteran from Mt. Airy, North Carolina. He is oblivious to the helicopters above and the many police cruisers closing in on the traffic around him. Jimmy is about to be propelled into a federal law enforcement world of shock and awe, hurt and misery. He will soon undergo his first Taser-gun experience.

None of it will help find Hillary.

Chapter Twenty-Six

A day before the New Hampshire vote and the polls are through the roof with Hillary as the overwhelming favorite. Platoons of TV lawyers are arguing the legality of holding the vote at all, since no one knows whether she is actually alive. This turns out to be irrelevant: one may surmise that she is living is the legal verdict.

A Washington, D.C., media-hound attorney, a self-described liberal named Jeffrey Toobin, makes an unfounded, unsupportable statement on a CNN roundtable - not exactly a reckless first for TV. He is crushed in return.

Toobin opines that maybe there is some "contrivance" going on with this kidnapping. Maybe someone "engineered" it to benefit Hillary. Other panelists, one of them the neurotic and girlish Dana Milbank from the Washington Post, are wide eyed at the suggestion. Unaware of the danger lurking in the weeds, Toobin treads on.

He says, "Look at the polls. A week ago she was falling fast, and now she is about to be the hands-down winner in New Hampshire? It's the sympathy vote. She hasn't even had to campaign." He is challenged immediately by a liberal reporter from Politico, who calls the comments "an outrage and a slander against Mrs. Clinton."

"Listen", says Toobin, "I'm not saying she did this herself. I'm just saying *maybe,* maybe some friends of hers or fans of hers orchestrated this and will let her go soon. It's only a thought, and probably wrong."

The Huffington Post punches and kicks him first, carrying a bannered story accusing Toobin of accusing Hillary of engineering her own kidnapping, burying his "maybe" and in later permutations dropping his "it's probably wrong."

In a flash, hungry for news about Hillary, *any* news, the story is then picked up by cable TV and the morning news shows, where pundits call it an "outrage" and slam Toobin for "blaming the victim because she is a woman," a theme Congresswoman Debbie Wasserman Schultz, in a white hot fury, spreads through the media in sound bites.

TV bookers begin to decline Toobin's offers to appear on their shows, some not taking his calls at all. Toobin's friends become fearful that he is considering suicide after the New York Times, in an editorial, calls him "a reckless ghoul" for comments about Hillary (that he didn't really make) and he learns that another leftwing attorney named Ron Kuby from New York has moved into his regular slot at CNN.

Hillary can hear the TV running in the next room. The "agents" have taken off her handcuffs after she swears to be better behaved, to be cooperative – and not to physically attack them.

She knows she is about to win New Hampshire from the overheard TV and is aware of the world hubbub over her kidnapping.

No genuine ransom notes have arrived to the FBI, or anywhere else – there have been a handful of phony letters and there has been no contact with the kidnappers.

The kidnappers themselves cook for her, mostly microwaved items like Hot Pockets and Eggo waffles and Red Baron Frozen pizza; or they bring in fast food. They wash her underwear. They iron her blouse and black suit pants. In the Georgetown Park mall they buy her comfortable boys' flannel pajamas to wear.

Otherwise, Hillary is often alone. She's asked for and received daily newspapers - the Washington Post, New York Times, and Washington Times. Wayne and Zipper don't know that the Washington Times is often critical of Hillary, though not since her kidnapping. The Times was sometimes so harsh towards her that her staff eliminated Times stories about her from their daily news-clips package.

She deeply enjoys reading the media tributes she now gets, particularly from Washington Times. There is something about being a victim that both soothes and smooth's your perspective, she thinks.

Hillary hasn't looked at a newspaper for years. She hasn't realized how much she misses reading them in the morning. She has relied for more than 20 years instead on bowdlerized news stories chosen and re-written for her by her earnest staffers.

Having the time to wander through the pages of a newspaper is a satisfying luxury, she realizes, chortling over the occasional story wherein one of her political enemies is metaphorically kicked in the teeth.

She laughs out loud to read that Joe Biden has insulted King Abdullah bin Abdilaziz of Saudi Arabia in a rambling monologue at a GLAD fundraiser in Minnesota. The event was closed to the press but open to someone's surreptitious microphone and recorder. (Joe opined how odd it was that the Saudis were still tormenting gay men in Arabia when "half the royal princes prefer boys, and sometimes even short camels, over girls." And then punctuated his statement with a series of loud guffaws, endlessly repeated on cable news shows.)

Well, here is an even weirder one, thinks Hillary. The story is about Supreme Court Justice Ruth Bader Ginsburg, almost 84 years old. She has been photographed at a Washington, D.C., sidewalk demonstration wearing a black beret heavy with political buttons, a Che Guevara T-shirt and ripped jeans adorned with black bumper stickers saying "A Woman Needs A Man Like A Fish Needs A Fucking Bicycle." Rumors of senility have swirled about her since the beginning of Obama's second term, but she has refused to step down, though liberals have pressured her to do so.

Justice Bader has shrunk a couple of inches over the years and is now 4'10". She was still recognized by a local TV reporter. She was parading in a picket line outside the National Geographic Headquarters Building on 17th Street, a few blocks from the White House. The protest was in support of striking janitors.

Justice Ginsburg talked to the reporter on camera and with considerable good cheer. The tiny woman said that she was indeed Ruth Bader Ginsburg but denied being on the Supreme Court. "I am General Counsel for the ACLU," she said, referring to a job she had left almost 40 years before. One of the striking janitors hustled her away.

She was admitted to George Washington Hospital later in the day, for "unidentified treatment" says the story, adding that she is expected to resign from the court. (A month later she does quit, citing health reasons. Liberals are furious at the timing, as it is too late for the lame duck Obama to replace her. The appointment will have to wait for a new president at the end of the year.)

The Republican National Committee is meeting at their headquarters and has put their own war-room into action, mostly on defense. Democrats, particularly representatives Alan Grayson and Debbie Wasserman-Schultz, are blaming Republicans for creating a "climate of hate" and waging a War on Women that is responsible for Mrs. Clinton's kidnapping as well as most other crimes against females in America.

Governor Cuomo of New York joins the chorus and Mayor De Blasio of New York City, Hillary's campaign manager for her New York senate race years before, holds a City Hall news conference with the parents of Trayvon Martin who are beginning a "prayer vigil" in Central Park for Mrs. Clinton.

"It is too late for Trayvon," says De Blasio. "But not too late for Hillary."

Chapter Twenty-Seven

Picking up on the widely circulated CNN roundtable story, and Jeffrey Toobin's media-skewed remarks, others are suggesting that perhaps Hillary Clinton has staged this whole circus herself and some cynics are saying so publicly. Mark Levin, on his syndicated radio show, points out other notorious disappearances of prominent women with a hidden agenda, to wit:

Reverend Aimee Semple McPherson, the famous evangelist at the Four Square Temple Church in Los Angeles did it in the 1920's. Turns out she was with a boyfriend, the lighting technician for her church, shacked up at the beach in Santa Barbara while the world agonized over her disappearance.

And maybe the famous author Agatha Christie faked it as well. She would never say where she had been for a couple of weeks in a famous disappearance in London and kept the secret to her death.

A talk show host named Alan Weismann in Albany, New York, picks up the "Maybe She did it to Herself" theme, suggesting her campaign was going under and she staged a life saving event to save it. Police arrest a dozen local feminists from NOW-Albany who show up outside the man's studio at the end of the broadcast and begin to assault him. One woman is carrying rope of such strength and length police believe they might have intended to lynch Weismann. As it is, he suffers a broken arm from being kicked while he lies on the ground.

Bill Clinton breaks down sobbing on an MSNBC show with Al Sharpton, who consoles him. "You must miss hearing her voice every day," says a sympathetic Sharpton, sniffling himself and hugging Bill.

"Oh, yes," says Bill, thinking to himself, "her frigging voice is the very *last thing* I'd miss. No way. That awful, whining grating voice. I like lots of things about Hill but the voice and the ankles, I don't fucking think so." But Bill is secretly ecstatic while hugging the simpering Sharpton.

Bill never has a thought that isn't political, that isn't designed to advance himself, or even Hillary, in some way. He can read those soggy tea leaves. He knows that if Hillary, as the ultimate victim, just stays away through February 16, she will cause a landslide in New Hampshire – and it will be a cakewalk to the Democratic Convention. And by God, this time she will win the nomination, and then the presidency. "She is going to have this race in the fucking bag," he thinks. "All of America loves a victim. We can milk this forever. Even Chelsea could someday ride into elected office on this."

"God. I hope she gets out alive before," he thinks. "Please God. That fucking Obama." Hillary should have won against him back in 2008. Eight years later and now it's about to go right up Obama's butt, a man about whom Bill

163

once said to Ted Kennedy, "In the old days he would be getting us coffee." Yes, if Hillary gets loose from the kidnappers or they find her alive, she is going to win. "This is a classic rat-fuck on Obama," thinks Bill, laughing on the inside.

Bill has moved temporarily to Hillary's house at 3067 Whitehaven Street in Washington, a mansion on a third of an acre right off Massachusetts Avenue, a stone's throw from the official residence of her political enemy Vice President Joe Biden. Bill was pushed to move to Whitehaven by Chelsea and a few other advisors who think he should be near the seat of government while the search for Hillary is on; and that it would look like sweet sensitivity to the public, who would imagine him sleeping in Hillary's bed every night, like a faithful old dog, until she returned home. Chelsea thinks that the added benefit is that it might keep him away from other women for a while.

Bill would much rather be in Chappaqua and near his office in Harlem, and the adoring crowds in tiny Manhattan restaurants.

Bill has been to the Whitehaven house so infrequently that he has forgotten how nice the place is. The rest of the country is swirling down the economic drain and Washington, D.C., where all the really stupid economic decisions are made, is booming. What an irony! "This place has got to be worth close to $10 million now," he thinks.

He is sitting in a spacious second floor guest room admiring the yellow cabbage rose wallpaper and how it matches the comforter on the queen size bed and the soft upholstered easy chair in which he now sits, and its fancy footstool, which he has pushed aside.

"Hillary has the taste of a frigging dog groomer," Bill thinks. He knows that her buddy Huma and other friends have been key to decorating Hillary's fancy pad, sometimes, very privately, called the Eagle's Nest. Among a few intimates, as a joke, it is called, in fractured German, Das Hillsteinhaus.

Bill's hands are soaking in a Lalique crystal bowl of soap and warm water. The bowl had been taken by Hillary from the White House when they moved out in 2008. He is about to get a manicure. His iPhone beeps once: a text message. He removes one hand, wipes it on his T-shirt, and looks at the message.

OMG, it is from Hillary. "Holy Fuck," says Bill aloud, as he silently reads. "Bill, I'm OK. They say they will let me go. Love, Hillary."

Bill's first thought: "the woman must have sent me ten thousand text messages and she has never signed one 'love.' It must be a code of some kind. I'll be damned if I can figure out what it means. Or maybe the text message is a complete phony, cooked up by the kidnappers to pacify me."

"What is it?" asks the smiling young woman kneeling on the $10,000 Aubusson carpet in front of him. She is wearing only a tiny polka dot thong, one of her small breasts resting on his knee as he gently caresses it with his thumb and forefinger.

She has interrupted herself while giving him the sweet-natured prelude to the manicure that he has asked for. "Is everything all right?"

"Sure, sure," Bill says. "Well, maybe not *all right* but certainly different," he thinks to himself.

"It's nothing. Go back to what you were doing," he mumbles. "Sure does feel good."

He leans back in the soft chair. "Man, I've gotta call the FBI or DHS about this text," he thinks, but he is teetering on the brink of drifting away, wrapped as he is in the arms of the Goddess Hedone, when the iPhone in his hand beeps again. "Such a joyless little buzzer," he thinks.

"Oh, don't stop," he signals, as he works the girl's nipple gently with one hand and his phone with the other.

"Damn," he thinks, reading the screen. It's Pinch Sulzberger, the whiny little trust fund doofus who runs the New York Times, as its chairman and publisher. "Runs it into the friggin' ground, is the way to describe it," chortles Bill, who has been watching the paper's value dwindle drastically over the years of Pinch's unsteady helmsmanship.

Carlos Slim, the Mexican tycoon, dropped a much-needed $250 million in cash into the company pot, diluting the Sulzberger's control of the stock of the company they have owned for more than 100 years. A busted rudder, no jib or boom, in a gale wind, as Teddy Kennedy had once described Pinch's leadership abilities to Bill. This was back when Kennedy was alive and they were still speaking, before Ted double-crossed Hillary for Obama. "Fucker," thinks Bill.

Well, Pinch loves Hillary. Just loves her. "If I didn't know better I'd suspect he might have once gotten into her pants. But, I do know better. He didn't," thinks Bill.

Pinch's father was Punch Sulzberger, also named Arthur. "Not a bad fellow," thinks Bill – "everybody seemed to like him, certainly more than this little jerk." But the downside was that Punch was a buddy of Monica Lewinsky's rich stepfather, Peter Straus, the Macy's heir, who had been married to Punch's cousin, Ellen Sulzberger for a lifetime. Ellen died, and Peter married Monica's mother. "Just around the time Louis Freeh, the little ingrate I appointed *myself*, sicced his FBI dogs on me over Monica."

Bill, totally cheerful, answers the call. "Hi Arthur, how are ya?" he asks.

"I just wanted you to know that The Old Gray Lady cares a whole lot about you and Hillary, Mr. President."

"Well, that's very nice, thank you Arthur," says Bill, thinking of Pinch's ex-wife, the artist, a pretty good lookin' little lady. Damn, he can't remember her name. The new wife isn't so hot.

"Well, sure, Mr. President. You know that when I say Old Gray Lady, I'm talking about our newspaper and its 126 smaller papers around the country, as well as all of our 3000 employees. We are in your corner, and Hillary's corner. We really do care, deeply."

"Three thousand employees, and getting smaller by the day through lay-offs and buy-outs," thinks Bill. It was more than 5,000 employees just a few years back.

"I've got one our top editors with me –you know Bruce Gelb?" says Pinch. (Bill doesn't, but they exchange howareyas regardless).

"Bruce has been in charge of the team covering this story, going into it deeply. Very deep, at least as deep as possible, as deeply as we are able, but the problem is there is just nothing new to cover."

"So, I was wondering if you have heard anything, any little lead you could pass on? We would pursue it for you, and for Hillary."

"Well, I really don't, Arthur. Sorry. I don't know anything you don't know," says Bill, not at all tempted to tell this little jerk about the text he just received from Hillary. "Ha, that would have given a real goose to the old 'Gray Lady,' handing them a huge banner headline. The gall of this guy, calling me to impress his sleazy editor. I don't think so."

"Stay in touch," Bill says as he hangs up the phone.

Chapter Twenty-Eight

At the Finding Hillary Task Force Headquarters there is an ongoing argument about whether to wait for Bill to contact them before contacting *him*. It has been at least 15 minutes since they were made aware of the text message to his phone, and Bill hasn't called them to pass it on.

"Give him another 15 minutes to call," says FBI Deputy Director Denny Walsh, who already has two agents sitting in an unmarked car on the street a few blocks down from the entrance to Whitehaven, 30 seconds from Hillary's house. They are standing by for word to approach the place and talk to Bill - or Bollocks, as they refer to him in radio transmissions - about the text message.

The NSA has told Walsh that Bill's cell phone is physically located at Hillary's Whitehaven house and that someone there has opened the message, presumably Bill. It is just that he hasn't yet called the special number given to him if he learns anything about Hillary, which is causing considerable consternation in the old Rubber Room.

Thirty minutes later, the two FBI agents are instructed by radio to approach the house and find out who has the phone. Bill's Secret Service detail is there, one agent is parked in front, and another opens the door and calls for the former President after he checks the FBI creds. A third agent is dozing, waiting to drive the "manicurist" home.

Bill comes down the broad main stairway. He looks a little sheepish. His gray shorts look damp. He says, "I just spilled some water on myself. What's going on?"

"It's about your phone, Mr. President. Did you receive a text from Mrs. Clinton," asks one agent.

"Ah, Jeez, I did. I forgot to call."

Despite still being missing and with no word at all of her whereabouts or condition, Hillary sweeps New Hampshire. It isn't even close. At a teary news conference Elizabeth Warren drops out of the race entirely, too traumatized by the whole affair. She says that Hillary's kidnapping is the death knell for civility in American politics, blaming the right for both the kidnapping and just about every other perceived ill in America. She then also resigns her Senate seat to return to being just another tenured, Native American law professor with a cushy Academy sinecure.

The other contenders, including Deval Patrick and Joe Biden, fall like human dominoes and abandon their respective efforts within a week of each other, out of public deference to the victimization of Hillary and the almost overwhelming public sympathy for her.

The road to the Democratic convention in August is open for Hillary, if Hillary is ever found alive. And if she's not, Biden signals to his aides and close associates that he has every intention of jumping back into the race.

171

The media, the New York Post specifically, prints inflammatory statements made by Biden to aides speculating that Hillary "might have cashed in her chips. When we find that out, I'm back in the race in a New York minute, f--k yeah," he is quoted as saying. The Post pounces on him for even considering it. It's time to focus on Hillary, they say, not on Joe Biden's opportunistic political ambitions.

The Obama Administration and the FBI have come up with no clues or sensible leads, not one – there has been really no progress at all, but Jeh Johnson at DHS continues to pretend there is. The media is unforgiving in its criticism of the Task Force. Thousands of tips have been called in, many of which have yet to be pursued. There simply isn't enough manpower.

In Frisco, Texas Earl "Fatha" Hines and Bobby Crandall are sitting on upturned buckets in a large field of sunflowers waiting for doves to fly over. Their side-by-sides, double-barreled shotguns, are cradled across their laps.

Fatha says, "Bobby, this is a Goddamned shame, a complete cluster-fuck. I can't believe this has happened. We two, you and me, are responsible for sending this woman right into the White House. We have just fucked the whole country, forever. Now I know I'll never tell my grandchildren about this."

Bobby says, "The FBI can't tie any tin-can to our bumper on this, right?"

Fatha says, "Not if those two boys keep their mouths shut. I told them not to call, not to do nothing. They are to let her go two days after New Hampshire and then use the extra 15 grand I gave them to drive that car to another state, sell it, keep the money —and take a couple week's vacation before they fly back to Texas to keep their mouths shut the rest of their lives."

Chapter Twenty-Nine

On Dent Place, Hillary pounds on the door. When One answers and asks what she wants, she replies, "How about getting me some iced tea? I'm so tired of Diet Coke. Besides, I think tea is better for me. Please make sure to get lemon with it. I like lemon. Understand?"

Zipper responds with a grumbling "Yes, Ma'am," grabs his wallet, and heads off to Roy Rogers. He returns in thirty minutes, unbolts her door, and steps into the room.

"Got your ice tea," he says, sounding cheery. "And, I brought you a 'Double-R burger' with some curly fries. And got your lemon."

"I don't like those 'Double-R' things, not three days in a row," she says, her voice rising. *"Please,* go back. Get me a 'Gold Rush Chicken' burger. No mayo. The Double-R's really taste like shit."

"Yes, Ma'am, I agree. The Double R used to be pretty good with all the cheese and ham on top of the burger. Good until your buddy Mrs. Obama put out all those nutrition rules and screwed them up. Totally changed how this stuff tastes."

"She's not my buddy, the bitch," says Hillary, irritated about the burger and guzzling some tea while she ponders the lemon slice. "I can't bear the woman. She is just awful."

"Michelle," she thinks. "Ah, what a self-inflated jerk she is." Last year Susan Rice pushed Hillary to have dinner with Michelle at Sushi Ko, a small Japanese place near Saks Fifth Avenue in Chevy Chase. Just the two of them, chewing diced squid in lettuce leaves and unidentifiable imponderables in rolled rice, while other diners stared, and they forced smiles for the audience's benefit through endless dumb small talk.

"What an irony," thinks Hillary, as One leaves, loudly bolting the door from outside: Hillary had noticed that Michelle's derriere could scarcely fit on the small and delicate Japanese chairs at Sushi Ko, and overhung it on the side like a giant marshmallow. "Her ass is the size of Plymouth Rock," Bill, ever the history buff, had once mused.

"It's *her* invitation and she sticks me with the frigging check," thinks Hillary.

"Look," she says, through the door. "I want to write a note to Chelsea to tell her I'm okay. Just a simple note. I know she's worried. You know she is too. Do either of you guys have children? If you had disappeared wouldn't you want someone you loved to know you were okay? I'll write it. You can read it and then mail it for me."

Zipper and Wayne trade glances. It IS a reasonable request. As long as they can read it and make sure she isn't saying anything to give away where she is or who is

175

holding her it will be fine. Fatha hadn't told them how to handle something like this, but it isn't out of line.

"Okay," says Wayne, "I'm fine with it as long as we can read it over carefully."

"Thank you," Hillary says in a politely condescending tone. "Now could you get me some paper and an envelope? I'd like to send something today. I don't want her worrying anymore than she already is."

Leaving Zipper with Hillary, Wayne trudges out the door. In a half an hour he is back, bringing a small box of plain cards and envelopes in a plastic bag with a CVS logo on the side. He crumples the bag and throws it in a wastebasket next to her desk.

"Give me one card and one envelope," she directs Wayne. "That's all I need. And can I have a few minutes alone while I write this? I just want to be able to think about my daughter and what she's going through."

Wayne obediently gives her a card and then an envelope. He finds a ballpoint pen in his bag in the front room, brings it to her, and then closes the door behind him as he leaves.

Hillary works quickly. She undoes the pen and pulls out the ink projectile. She then squeezes lemon juice onto her clean coffee cup saucer on the top of the desk. Dipping the opposite end of the ink cartridge into the lemon juice she writes the Dent Street address onto the bottom of the card. She also writes, "I'm here. basement. Two men." Then she flaps the card in the air, drying the lemon juice.

When it is dry she writes on the card in big bold letters: "I'm okay, Darling. Do not fret. They're treating me well. I hope to see you very soon. Love, Mom."

Then she addresses the envelope to "C.C., Box Holder" and writes out a post office box in Springfield, Virginia, about 15 miles south of Washington. Hillary picks the CVS bag out of the wastebasket. There is a receipt inside with the CVS address on Wisconsin Avenue which she knows is likely very close to Dent Place, the address on the electric bill. The Dent Place address is still good, she thinks, so happy it brings tears to her eyes, or at least almost.

She calls Wayne back in. As he enters she wipes an invisible tear from her eye and tries to express some motherly emotion. "This is so hard," she says, blotting her eyes. "Chelsea is my everything. I just want to be sure she knows I'm okay."

She hands the unsealed card to Wayne. He reads it quickly, noting the part that says, "They're treating me well."

"At least she isn't complaining," he thinks to himself.

He hands it back and then she gives him the envelope. "It goes to a post office box," she explains. "Chelsea uses a post office box that only a few of us know, just as Bill and I use one that she knows. That way we have some mail that is private."

It makes sense to Wayne - public figures do need some things to be private. and that was a good way to do it. Use a post office box instead of your real physical address.

Wayne hands the envelope back to Hillary and she slips the note inside and seals it.

"Do you think you can mail this today?" she asks.

"Yes, Ma'am," he replies. "Today. Before they pick it up at 5. She might have it in her box tomorrow."

Indeed, it is in the box the next day. But it isn't going to Chelsea, who is never to learn of it.

Chapter Thirty

Sometime after 3 in the afternoon on the following day, Li Kai Fong, a long-serving Ministry of State Security intelligence officer posted undercover as an economic attaché to the People's Republic of China Embassy opens the post office box at a Mailboxes R Us in Springfield, Virginia, as he does once every day, six days a week.

He is humming a popular Beijing song, roughly translated, as "I Want to Bind Your Feet With the Ribbons of My Heart." He shuffles through the junk mail. Ah, as he has hoped, there in the jumble of carpet cleaning ads and fliers from Pizza Hut is a personal letter.

Someone has written in ballpoint pen "For C.C." and the PO Box number and address. He carries it unopened to his car, protected by some junk mail. With a penknife from his automobile key chain, after first pulling on some Abbot Labs medical gloves (made in China), he carefully slits open the envelope and removes the letter with the tip of the knife.

Fong has worked with Hillary off and on for many years helping facilitate the delivery of money to Bill's campaigns, beginning way back in Arkansas, up through his presidential races, and then smaller amounts to her Senatorial campaign - 'walking around money,' she calls it - and much more to her last presidential race against Obama. He is now working to wash a couple of million

179

more in cash from China itself and parts of Africa where China has investments and influence, as Hillary heads to the Democratic Party Convention next summer. It wasn't lawful, Hillary had once told Fong, but it was every bit as fair as those damned Republican PACs and people like those fucking Koch brothers who support the conservatives.

"Mrs. Clinton," Fong chuckles to himself. He has spent much private time with her, and his grasp of the American vernacular language and its vulgarities is top drawer. "For an elderly, married woman - she must be close to 70," he thinks, "she has a very bad mouth."

Hillary and Bill have long been convinced that having a clandestine relationship with China could prove beneficial in his, and then her, long-term political careers: a careful, discrete back-channel relationship that could address and sometimes ameliorate problems made great sense. They had jointly decided this, though it was Hillary who first sold it to Bill when he was running for governor and she was approached by a Chinese-American businessman with a lot of cash to throw around. The relationship grew from there.

Hillary never intended to sell or give away any classified U.S. secrets and never did, even as Secretary of State, a period when she had many chances to further her relationship with the PRC and during a time when Fong began pushing her for answers to policy-planning issues at their infrequent personal meetings, questions which she invariably deflected.

Selling out her country, at least directly, wasn't in her DNA, but rule-breaking of any other kind to further her overweening ambition and salve her deep insecurities is. This attitude dominates her subconscious; it is in her blood and bones, saturating every fiber of her body.

It must be genetic, she thinks, as she can see it so clearly in Chelsea, who has turned into quite a little self-serving operator herself. Just look at how she pushed the attorney Doug Band, Bill's butt boy for all those years, right out of the lucrative picture and grabbed a piece of the Clinton foundation (now the $250-million Bill, Hillary and Chelsea Clinton Foundation), buying an $11 million Manhattan apartment for herself (in the same four-unit building –The Whitman at 2 East 26th, which stretches an entire city block. The singer J. Lo paid $22-million for her penthouse in the same building, with its grass croquet court (called a 'pitch' on her 3,000 square foot deck. Chelsea has been pulling down $600,000 a year for doing nada at NBC. The girl is amazing, remarkable, Hillary thinks, and laudable to the extreme.

Chelsea is much closer to Bill, or always had been throughout childhood when Hillary was busy and his maternal instincts were stronger frankly. "But she is now, as an adult approaching middle age, very much like her mother," thinks Hillary proudly.

181

Being able to communicate directly and secretly to the PRC if she becomes President could prove beneficial for many reasons. The Chinese think the exact same thing.

Li Kai Fong reads the card and then holds it up to the sunlight. He sniffs it. He thinks he detects the odor of lemon across the bottom of the paper. Taking out a small flashlight with an intense beam, he applies some heat to the card by pressing the light against it. The lemon message rises clearly out of the fiber. The address where she is being held is in his hands: 3237 Dent Place, Northwest, Washington, D.C. It is her handwriting. He looks at the postmark on the envelope. She seems to be okay, at least as of yesterday.

Li pulls out of the parking lot and makes his way over to I-395 North, into Washington. He needs to get to the Embassy. He calls ahead as he drives, telling the ambassador's secretary that he must see the boss, chop chop. He looks at his watch. It is now 3:15am in Beijing.

In 30 minutes he is sitting in a chair across from Ambassador Zhang Yesui. The sun spills late afternoon light through the ambassador's tall office windows, filtered by the leaves of two towering tulip maple trees nearby on the lawn.

Fong tells what he has learned to Ambassador Zhang and to the PRC Intel Chief, his own boss, Lieutenant General

Han Wu. He shows them the envelope and note, now in a plastic sleeve.

(Later, embassy techs will have the papers checked for fingerprints and DNA residue. They will find Hillary's thumbprint on the card from their database, and from their own U.S. Military Print Archive they will identify two latent prints, thumb and forefinger, belonging to a former E-5 U.S. Army Military Policeman named Wayne B. Wayne, last known address in Texas. By then they know from the U.S. media that he is one of the two kidnappers.)

The ambassador's secretary dictates a message from the ambassador to a code clerk, who has arrived from the secure floor above. It is sent on the highest priority top-secret digital channel, per protocol, directly to the Foreign Minister in Beijing, with urgent copies to three other men, all members of the Standing Committee of the 25-member Politburo: First Ranked Xi Jinping, General Secretary of the Communist Party of the People's Republic of China, and president of the country; 2nd Ranked Cui Kequiang and 3rd Ranked Zhang Dejian.

The Standing Committee makes all important decisions in the PRC. The 25 Politburo members meet once a month. There are 10 Standing Committee members, and they meet once a week or on an ad hoc basis for emergencies. The cable carries instructions that all four leaders are to be awakened and delivered the message by hand, with a request for an immediate reply.

The encrypted cable reads:

> *"We have learned late this afternoon of the exact, repeat exact, Washington, D.C., location of former Secretary of State Hillary Clinton. She is being held in the basement of a private house in the Georgetown section. As of yesterday she was unharmed. She is presumed to be held by two kidnappers. The U.S. authorities apparently do not have this information. Also, presumably, they do not know that we know. We recommend immediate covert action by this embassy to free her. Please advise,*
>
> *Respectfully, Zhang Yesui, Ambassador."*

They receive a response in one hour, decrypted and delivered to the ambassador's office where Fong, General Han and the ambassador wait.

It is signed by Foreign Minister Wang Yi, also a member of the powerful PRC CP Central Committee, and has the full concurrence of General Secretary Xi Jinping and the two other contacted (and awakened) ranking members of the Politburo Standing Committee. It reads, in full:

> *"Rescue her! Do it surreptitiously. Do not get caught. Do not tell the U.S. we know where she is. They will demand to know how we know. We must not jeopardize our secret 'relationship' with her. She will soon be their leader. Keeping her alive and safe is a PRC CP priority. Fu"*

Fu is a popular word in China. It means good luck.

The National Security Agency, America's premier covert intelligence gathering agency, reads both of these messages within minutes. The sophisticated Chinese diplomatic code was broken by NSA cryptographers in 2015 and has been highly productive. This is a closely kept secret.

The news in these two messages, to and from the PRC Foreign Ministry and Ambassador Zhang, is startling, to understate it. The NSA director, Vice Admiral Ainsworth Baggott, is entertaining his wife and her former college roommate, who is visiting, at NSA's Headquarters. He asks them to excuse him as he heads down the hall to a small Secure Compartmented Information Facility (SCIF) – a space that is virtually impossible to penetrate by technical means, and in which the most classified of material is stored or worked with or in which very sensitive discussions or briefings are held.

The two women have just returned to his office after a tour of a tiny portion of the NSA's grey/black, perfectly square Headquarters building (known officially as OPS2A and by non-NSA neighbors as the "Black Rubik's Cube"). It is located at Fort Meade, Maryland, 18 miles southwest of Baltimore.

The Headquarters and its adjacent building are covered in dark one way glass lined with copper sheeting to prevent the escape of signals and sounds to any interested ears or devices outside. They contain three million square feet of floor space.

The women have been drinking tea in the Director's spacious blue-carpeted office, the three of them sitting in stuffed easy chairs of grey and rust tweed, across from a long wooden desk, a conference table with 12 leather chairs and a wall of tastefully arranged plaques, photos and awards.

The directorate building, and a lower rectangular building, contain 20,000 to 30,000 employees (the figures, like NSA's annual budget, are classified), some of them working in a huge ten-acre underground annex next to, and partly under, the dark buildings.

Three officers, two of them fluent in Mandarin, physically deliver the decrypted messages to the Director's office. They are sent by his secretary to the SCIF where the Director sits at a small table. The senior person of the three, a middle-aged woman in a black dress and a blue turquoise necklace, reads the messages aloud to the director after handing him a printed, translated copy.

The NSA Director thanks them and picks up a direct line to the FBI Director from a secure phone on the table.

"We need to meet immediately," he says.

Chapter Thirty-One

The front doorbell rings at the Dent Place house at 6:30pm. Wayne Wayne looks out from the living room curtains. The wrought iron gate from the sidewalk to the 15-foot long front walk is open. A young woman holding a paper bag stands on the landing outside the door.

Wayne tucks his .38 caliber snub-nosed Chief's Special Colt revolver into his trousers' waistband and pulls his red flannel shirt down over it. A pretty Asian girl is standing on the landing. She holds out the bags and says, "I have your order." It is Katie Wang, who smiles broadly. She is lovely, thinks Wayne, not a word common in his everyday vocabulary.

"No one here ordered anything," Wayne replies. "Sorry."

"I am sorry for mistake. You are sure you not order?" She is using her faulty English.

Wayne is holding open the glass-paneled storm door. Katie drops the bag. It hits the polished wood floor hard. Won Ton soup, brown sliced mushrooms and some noodles (hand made by Chief Wang) gather on the polished wood floor and lap against the edge of the living room rug.

"Damn," says Wayne. "Stay here," and he runs to the small kitchen, returning with a roll of paper toweling and a sponge. Katie is leaning on the black iron railing on either side of the landing. She is crying.

"Wait, wait," says Wayne, who is cleaning the mess, or at least pushing it away from the carpet. "It's OK, just an accident. You didn't mean it."

She looks up at him, her black eyes bright and shiny with tears, her gorgeous lips parted, showing perfect white teeth. He puts his long arm out and around her shoulder. "Missy, it is all right. It's not a problem. Smile, don't be upset. Please don't cry."

"They will be so angry with me at restaurant. This our first week of deliveries. I know I lose job."

"How much is the freight for this?" asks Wayne. She shows him the bill. "$24.95." "Here," he says, pulling two twenties from a roll in his pocket. "You keep the change. No one will be the wiser."

"Oh you are so very nice man and so kind. Thank you. Thank you." She stands on her toes and kisses his cheek.

"Can I bring you a free meal? Yes? Please? I will bring Tsin-Tsin Chow Mein, our specialty and some Colonel Tso's Chicken. Yes? How many people?"

Wayne is touched and almost weak in the knees from the kiss.

"Well there are three of us," he says.

188

"Three men?" she asks. "Sometimes women not like Colonel Tso's - too spicy hot."

"Two guys and a girl. My aunt," says Wayne. "If anybody would like it spicy it would be Aunt Angelina. Yes ma'am. So let Colonel Tso be Colonel Tso. Spicy it is."

"I come back tomorrow, maybe around 7:30 be OK?" she says. "If you promise to answer door so I see you again." And she smiles shyly.

"That would be perfect," he says.

She walks down the walk and stops at the open gate. She looks back over her shoulder at Wayne, throwing him another modest but happy smile, turning her body just enough so he can see her full breasts outlined against her polo shirt. He watches her get into a small, old Dodge Dart with magnetic signs on the side saying, "Tsin-Tsin Delivery – Georgetown."

Chapter Thirty-Two

At the Task Force Headquarters, Homeland Security Chief Jeh Johnson, FBI Director James Comey, Secretary of State John Kerry, CIA director Michael Vickers and White House Chief of Staff Wallace McNulty are seated and waiting as NSA Director, Admiral Ainsworth Baggott, enters the room. Baggott is formidably smart. He has a PhD in physics from MIT and is a former head of the CIA's Directorate of Science and Technology -Clever Spy Gadget Central.

Baggott stands behind a chair at the head of the table. An elderly female stenographer sits at its far end with her fingers resting on her Stenotype machine. She can deliver instant, real-time transcription at a speed of 320 typed words per minute.

No staff is in the dozen or more chairs lined up around the painted, pale blue walls.

Secretary Kerry's presence was not requested, nor wanted, since this is an intelligence agency/law enforcement matter, not one of diplomacy or for the State Department. But no one questions him.

Kerry is widely disliked and very aware of it. Jokes are made behind his back. He is frequently called "OBN" – which was popularized by Washington talk show host Chris Plante on WMAL radio. Plante calls Kerry, "Old

Bolt Neck" because of his vague resemblance to a movie Frankenstein, ever since his face was so thoroughly surgically lifted by plastic surgeons a couple of years ago. Kerry's face is now so tight he can barely laugh without making his ears wiggle. It very much resembles a horses' leather feed bag in shape, size and smoothness. If Kerry were light green in color he would look like Shrek's smaller brother.

Today, in typical overbearing fashion, he has had a large cardboard box of handmade, "New England Cider Doughnuts" sent from a store in Rutland, Vermont - 50 of them wrapped in a fancy cloth liner, to the Task Force Headquarters main conference room. They're all delivered at some likely astronomical cost charged to his wife who he calls "Terr-ay-za" - Teresa Hines, who walked away with $400 million in Heinz 57 Variety bucks from her husband's Pittsburgh catsup fortune after he was killed when a helicopter struck his small plane and it crashed. When Kerry married Teresa he had, literally, a negative net worth. Now he can't spend money fast enough. The fancy doughnuts are typical of the many reasons these other men think OBN is a pompous ass and don't like him.

Admiral Baggott of NSA runs the meeting. Baggott has strong management skills as well as excellent technical abilities. He has weathered various NSA domestic evesdropping scandals. He has the admiration of his subordinates and contemporaries and most of the Congress.

"Gentlemen, we've been code breaking the high security diplomatic channel at the Chinese Embassy for the past two years - decrypting their primary backchannel link - the ambassador here in Washington to the Foreign Ministry in Beijing. The direct line. It's the highest order diplomatic channel there is."

Baggott, who loathes sharing secrets like this with anyone, even the President, announces sternly. "I tell this to you now because it relates directly to the kidnapping of Mrs. Clinton." He looks around the room. He has everyone's rapt attention.

"Last night we decrypted a message that indicates the PRC Embassy knows exactly where Hillary is. They have someone in their Embassy who has communicated clandestinely with Hillary for a number of years. Apparently he received a letter from her yesterday, postmarked the previous day, stating she was alive and well. She's being held somewhere in Georgetown."

There is stunned silence from the men around the table. John Kerry puts his head in his hands, and moans softly. He is thinking of how quickly and how far away from his predecessor, the annoying Hillary, he can get when the news about her secret Chinese links hit the press.

"We knew that a high level U.S. political figure had a clandestine relationship with the Chinese, but we didn't know who it was," says the Admiral, looking discomforted. The source's code name was "BISCUIT" earlier in the year. Then they changed it to "SLING".

"The Chinese Ministry of Security often changes code names of sources and agents for operational security reasons, so we attach no special significance to this. Regardless, we do now know who BISCUIT and SLING are for certain - our former First Lady, the former New York Senator, the former Secretary of State: Hillary Clinton."

"Why the hell is he looking at me?" thinks Kerry. "I don't have anything to do with this or with the Chinese." He pretended to look at his scratchpad. "If this gets out Teresa will hit the roof. She has never liked Hillary. And she'll be all over me for not knowing about it," he thought. Kerry was deeply afraid of his wife.

Baggott continues, "She has been using the PRC to launder foreign campaign contributions for both her and her husband, we believe for years, based on the cable traffic."

"Holy shit," says the CIA Director.

Baggott takes a swallow from a bottle of grape-flavored Propel water and continues after wiping his lips on his uniform sleeve.

"The good news is this, if you could call it that: we don't think she has traded intelligence or inside information to them. We don't believe she has committed espionage for them. I say this because we have read encrypted cable traffic complaining about BISCUIT/SLING's unwillingness to reciprocate with classified information in return for all the embassy efforts in washing campaign money for her and her husband. It clearly irritates the Politboro. "Such a one way street, with SLING," said the Foreign Minster to the ambassador here, and that was just two months ago.

"But the Chinese are playing a long game and Hillary may well become the president. They seem to be counting on it. That's when the pressure on her to become their Larry Chin* will intensify. I would say this would begin to happen between the election in November, assuming she wins, and her inauguration.

"So we know from the cables that they know where she is. What the cables didn't say is the address where the kidnappers have hidden her. The Embassy didn't cite the address, probably because it was gratuitous and would mean nothing to Beijing."

But the absence of the address means everything to the frustrated U.S. officials at the Task Force Headquarters.

Baggott says, "Somehow, according to the ambassador's message, she sent a note to her contact. She told him she's fine and being treated well. We believe Hillary is still alive, that she's probably safe, and that the Chinese Embassy, of all 'sniffer dogs,' can lead us to her."

"The Chinese ambassador asked the Ministry what to do. The answer was to not tell the U.S. government anything but to try to facilitate her escape. Make it look like she somehow did it on her own. Let her find her own way to safety. Just get her away from the kidnappers and leave no trace back to the PRC."

"Ambassador Zhang indicated he could get an agent to Hillary's location to make a surreptitious assessment. He provided no details. Just prior to this meeting now, I shared all of this, everything we know, with FBI Director Comey. We continue to monitor the channel and will immediately report any new traffic."

footnote: Larry WuTai Chin, a PRC agent, infiltrated the CIA where he worked as a translator. He passed CIA secrets to the PRC from 1952 to 1985 when he was caught. He offered to cooperate with the USG and committed suicide in his jail cell in Alexandria, Virginia, the day his debriefing was to begin.

As Admiral Baggott sits down, CIA Director Michael Vickers rises to speak. "He is without a doubt this Administration's biggest bootlicker," thinks the Admiral.

"Gentlemen, kudos to Admiral Baggott for his highly credible information assessment. We don't believe the Chinese are testing us or trying to run a deception operation. There's no motive. We at CIA weren't previously aware of the intelligence operation NSA is using to get this information, but after our discussions with Admiral Baggott over the past hour, our own analysis indicates it's probably pure. That is, the Chinese have no idea whatsoever that we have broken into the link and are able to do real-time decryption of their traffic. Our baseline analysis is that the Chinese do in fact have genuine information about Hillary's presence. The CIA will continue to monitor our own sources to see what else we might learn. Thank you."

FBI Director Comey speaks. "The Bureau is on this. We have maximized our surveillance on the ChiCom Embassy's known intelligence officers. They have a busy presence here, but we think we have all of them identified. We're putting watch-teams on almost every damned employee they have here. I've brought in another hundred bureau agents from New York, Philadelphia, and Baltimore. We intend to miss nothing – and hopefully one of the surveillance subjects will lead us to Hillary."

"The note from Mrs. Clinton with the address of where she is held, last we knew, was in the Chinese ambassador's office. Perhaps it is still there, or possibly it is in his safe. We considered a black bag job on the chancery. We did make such an extra-legal entry there a couple of years ago and were almost caught. We'd like to try again but it's too risky under the present circumstance."

CIA Director Vickers is toying with his spectacles, cleaning them with his tie after breathing heavily on each wire-circled glass.

"I'll reiterate that although the Chinese know something we don't, that doesn't mean they're involved. It just means they know something. The fact they don't want to tell us doesn't mean a lot either, other than the fact they don't want to burn Mrs. Clinton by letting us know that they have some relationship with her, as strange as that appears to be."

Vickers had replaced James Clapper at the Pentagon subsequent to Clapper's moving up to become the nation's top intelligence professional, a position from which he was ultimately retired in the aftermath of lying to Congress about NSA surveillance. Vickers was later quietly instrumental in expediting his predecessor John Brennan's departure from the CIA. Sources told FBI director Comey that Vickers had his nose so far up Obama's butt they had to promote him to get it unstuck.

Kerry jumps in. "Holy shit! The last thing we want is any confrontation with the Chinese. We've got enough problems as it is." Everyone ignores Old Bolt Neck and his irrelevant whining.

Director Comey speaks up. "Here's what I think. Let Admiral Baggott's people continue to monitor the backchannel link and update us. Meanwhile NSA and the Bureau will pick up every other communication we can between the Embassy and any of its people wandering around town. I already have every bureau Chinese linguist involved. The more real-time we are, the better off we are."

"If we have a sense of where they're going to take some sort of action, let's keep way back unless we know for certain Hillary is in danger. The Chinese don't want her hurt. It's possible the kidnappers don't want that either, although we can't be sure. We need to be involved, but from a distance that doesn't alert the Chinese or worse, get in their way."

White House Chief of Staff Wallace McNulty finally pops in. "I'll brief the President on what's happened here. I recommend we be back here in four hours with thoughts, ideas, and plans. Let's get ready for action. Let's save Hillary."

"Save Hillary," Secretary Kerry softly says as he stands and pushes his chair back. "Save Hillary." He would like to smile, but he can't. It makes his ears move.

Chapter Thirty-Three

The following day, at 6pm, Wayne and Zipper, old One and Two, knock on Hillary's door in the basement. She has the bedside light on but flips on the overhead chandelier to brighten the room.

Zipper and Wayne come in. They are about to announce that they are going to let her go. They plan to drive her somewhere outside the city and leave her. Zipper has scouted out the Montgomery Mall in Maryland, an upscale shopping center with close to 200 stores. It is on Democracy Boulevard near Interstate 270 and the Capital Beltway. He has decided the outside entrance to the Pottery Barn store looks like a good spot to release her.

Hillary is standing by the bed in the pajamas Zipper has bought her. They have baseballs, bats and catcher's mitts on them. She has grown fond of them and wears them much of the time.

"Mrs. Clinton" begins Zipper, "we are going to release you. Yes, we are going to let you go. We are going to do it later tonight. We'll take you out to Maryland to a mall. We don't want to tie you up or use a blindfold or a gag or something like that. We just want you to drive out there with us and let us release you. We've never intended to hurt you. We've even come to kind of like you, or at least respect you. You are a tough woman. You've proven it. Will you just go quietly to the mall with us? I'll drive. One will be in the back with you in case you get some idea to escape before we get there, which would be pretty dumb since we are letting you go. You can get help there right away after were gone."

Zipper is carrying a plain paper sack with handles. What looks like soft brown fur is gathered at the top. He puts it on the bed. It is the Angelina Jolie mask and wig from the Memphis magic shop. "You got your pet monkey in there, Mr. Two?" asks Hillary, when she sees the mound of brown hair.

Zipper, whose sense of humor is a little thin sometimes, says, "Oh no. It is an Angelina Jolie mask. We want you to wear it in the car when we drive out of here in an hour or two. We don't want anyone recognizing you or your blonde hair."

Hillary pulls out the rubber mask. It has heavily red painted lips and wavy dark brown hair that looks real.

"You're serious, right? So where is Brad Pitt, to keep me company in the back seat?"

Hillary decides to go along with this lunacy.

"That would be fine, great, Mr. Two. Now, why do I know in my heart that this is your idea?" She is holding Angelina up by the hair, like a Sioux warrior displaying a trophy scalp .

Zipper is flattered. He smiles broadly.

Hillary is looking at Zipper. What a fucking moron this guy is, she is thinking, but decides to tone herself down a notch in hopes they really mean it about letting her go. It's an effort, but she says sweetly, "Okey dokey, artichokey," using her most favorite phrase. But then she adds, "Mr. Two, sometimes I wonder about you. Notice that that rhymes, by the way," she says. "Of course I'll sit there quietly. What do you think - I'm going to jump out somewhere while we're driving and get flattened by a Greyhound bus? Really, I hope after I'm gone and this is over you get some perspective in your miserable, pathetic life."

She rethinks this and adds, insincerely, "I've begun to like you both, at least a little, myself."

"Okay, Mrs. Clinton," Wayne joins in. "By the time you can get help we'll be gone, on our way to Maine and back to Canada," he says, winking at Zipper and hoping that will throw her off a bit when she is debriefed by the cops.

"Mrs. Clinton," Zipper continues, "I know you're tired of Roy Rogers. We'll try Chinese tonight for our last meal together. They are going to deliver in a while."

At 7:30pm there is a knock at the door.

"It's our food," exclaims Wayne. "I'll get it." He bounds up the stairs while Hillary goes into the bedroom and then on into the bathroom to wash her hands. She closes the bedroom door and then the bathroom door behind her.

Wayne peers out the peephole. It's the beautiful Chinese girl, just as he has hoped. He opens the door slowly and greets her with a big smile.

"How much do I owe you?" he asks politely.

"Oh, no. Remember, this free," she replies, stuffing the warm bags of food into his hands – the food is just plain rice in untraceable containers. She reaches around behind her back and pulls out a silenced 9mm Makarov, points it at his forehead, and pulls the trigger. Wayne crumbles to the floor, a small amount of blood oozing from the neat hole just below his hairline.

Stepping over him, she hears Zipper downstairs say "Come on, man. We're hungry!"

Quietly she goes down the stairs. Zipper is sitting in one of the chairs, his back to her as he watches TV. She doesn't see anyone else but she does hear a toilet flush behind a closed door. She walks in front of Zipper, who starts to bring up his hands, and she places a bullet in his forehead as well.

She doesn't see or hear Hillary and in fact isn't even positive it is her behind the door. It doesn't matter. She has done her work and now needs to get away.

She bounds up the stairs, picks up the sack of rice from the floor, unscrews the silencer from the pistol, throws the gun on the floor, steps over Wayne's body, and closes the door behind her. From below, Hillary listens to these odd noises and shuffling from above. Then nothing. She doesn't yet realize it but she is free.

As Katie rounds the corner of Dent Place and 34th, she spots a marked D.C. Metropolitan Police car. A sole officer is sitting behind the wheel, his overhead light illuminating his face. He seems to be eating. He looks up and sees her. She makes a snap decision. Seek diversions, she had learned at spy school in Beijing.

"Officer, officer," she yells to him through his open window. "Something is going on at 3237 Dent Place. I was delivering food and I heard people yelling, maybe even a gunshot. I don't know." She points, "That big yellow house!"

Patrolman Rodney Williams, the 46-year-old officer with 25 years on the force and six months away from a comfortable retirement with lifetime benefits has a mouth full of his mother Stella's Glazed Apple Brunch cake, painted with walnuts and brown sugar, still warm in the aluminum foil. Damned good stuff, he thought. She has packed two big slices in a sack and he is savoring it with a large cup of Starbuck's Mocha Latte (which he paid for at the 50% "police price") when this snappy looking Oriental lady runs up on him yelling about some kind of crime.

"Check it out, Rodney, that's your job," he says to himself.

Without asking for any of her information, like her name and address, Officer Williams cranks up the car, makes a U-turn, and drives 100 feet over to 3237, double parking and leaving his flashing light on. The Chinese woman walks away and disappears down the sidewalk.

As Williams pulls up to the Dent Place address he can see that the front door is open. Somebody is standing in the doorway, leaning against the jamb. A woman, her hands partly covering her face. She appears to be wearing winkled pajamas.

"Stay where you are," he orders, climbing out of his car and approaching slowly, his square black Glock automatic pointed towards the door. As he edges from the darkness into the light, the woman lowers her palms from her face. She looks familiar.

"My God,' he thinks, as he approaches. "She looks just like Hillary Clinton, without make up! Holy shit!"

The woman, who is barefoot, stumbles down the steps, holding the rail.

"Ma'am, are you okay? What's happened here?"

"I don't know," is the calm reply. "I'm Hillary Clinton. I've been kidnapped. The kidnappers are dead. Both of them. Dead as frigging doornails. I don't know who did it. I didn't see what happened. All I know is that I want to get the fuck out of here."

Chapter Thirty-Four

Hillary Clinton Alive, Safe, Found Wandering in Georgetown.   Kidnappers Dead.   Both Texans. Right-wing Connections Being Explored. One Was Active Shriner.   DC Policeman Hailed As Hero.

—   Banner headline in Washington Post

As soon as Officer Williams recognizes with certainty that it is Hillary, he helps her down onto the cool grass while he secures the site.   He doesn't sense any danger.   Mrs. Clinton has said there were two kidnappers and they are both dead.   He'll call for backup once he's had a quick but careful look at the place.

He moves slowly towards the front door, both of his arms extended straight following their two-handed grip on his pistol, right hand index finger next to the trigger, safety off.   There, on the living room rug, against the stubby leg of an upholstered footstool, he spots a gun and, lying on his right side near it, the crumpled body of a young man in blue jeans and a faded red flannel shirt.

A thin rivulet of blood, as narrow as taut string, has run down the side of the dead man's forehead from a hole two inches above his dark eyebrows; it follows his hairline and forms a tiny pool, the circumference of a nickel, on the expensive yellow carpet.

Rodney deftly leans over, picks the gun up and puts it in his waistband. He uses his hand-held radio to call in.

"This is Officer Williams, car 287, Second Precinct. I'm at 3237 Dent Place, near 34th street, in Georgetown. I've got Mrs. Clinton here. Hillary Clinton. *MRS. HILLARY CLINTON!*" He shouts this last, the ramifications of his incredible good fortune fast dawning on him.

"She's safe, safe. Two suspects are dead. I'VE GOT HER! "

He isn't actually sure two people are dead. He's seen one who looks dead from a few feet away and she has told him they are dead. He is taking her word for it, but does think if someone else were there they would either be dead or severely wounded. Otherwise they would have fled.

Hillary is now lying in the grass on her back, knees pulled up, hands across her chest. It is cold but she doesn't feel it. Waves of relief run up and down her body. It's over. She is safe, her naked toes caressing the grass.

Officer Williams kneels beside her and speaks. "It's okay now, Mrs. Clinton," he says. He grasps her cold hand and says, "I'm officer Rodney Williams. From the Washington D.C., Metropolitan Police Department, Second Precinct. Rodney B. Williams. I'm the one who found you."

"That's nice to know, officer. I'm so glad that I'm safe and that you have rescued me," she says with a slight edge in her voice that goes unnoticed by B-Rod. "Now how about getting me out of here? I want to go home."

As she is speaking, sirens are screaming their approach from every direction, converging on 3237 Dent Place.

Williams turns away from Hillary, pulls the Makarov pistol from his waistband and drops it into his pocket. The wheels in his head are spinning in overdrive; synapses are firing like miniature machine guns. He doesn't know what has gone down here but Mrs. Clinton has just said she doesn't know what happened either - didn't see a thing.

"Play it cool, close to my bulletproof vest, and with a little luck maybe I can parlay this into something very good - very good for Officer Rodney B. Williams."

As the first squad cars arrive with screeching tires and flashing lights, officers begin running to the scene. Many have their weapons drawn. Some of them jump behind their cars and point guns at Williams and Hillary. Others run up to bushes on the neighbors' lawns and do the same.

"In there," Williams shouts, pointing to the house. Wayne's crumpled body can be seen just inside the glass storm door.

Two officers timidly approach the house and enter. Their guns are drawn. After a few minutes there is a shout. "Another one down here in the basement. Dead, too."

A very fat female officer gets a blanket out of the trunk of her car and puts it around Hillary's shoulders. "The ambulance will be here in a moment, Mrs. Clinton," she says. "In just a minute."

Hillary lets out a low grunt and sits up. The police are already running yellow tape to mark off the area. Some onlookers from the neighborhood are gathering outside the taped boundary and two TV camera crews and a satellite truck have arrived, driving up on the sidewalk at the corner. The police keep all of them back.

A senior lieutenant arrives on the scene, pushing other officers aside, then a captain arrives and does the same to the lieutenant until the chief arrives and pushes everyone else to the side.

The Metropolitan Police Second District Headquarters building has emptied out, all but for one elderly sergeant at the front desk, as officers rushed pell mell to Dent Place – and a chance to be on TV at an historic event. The last of them are two policewomen in yellow helmets and black Spandex tights, from the Mountain Bike Night Patrol, pedaling furiously down Wisconsin Avenue, dodging auto traffic.

"What happened here? Who was first on the scene?"

"Me," Officer Williams replies. "Me. It was definitely me."

The two lieutenants, the captain and the chief make their way quickly over to Hillary. They want to make certain she knows each is present and accounted for.

Officer Williams, now barely more than a bystander as senior officers begin arriving, makes his way up the two steps to the door. He looks at Wayne lying on the rug and makes his way in. He can hear a few officers downstairs, so he heads there. The overall scene hasn't yet been secured. A young Asian officer tries to stop him, but he says, more sharply than he ever usually spoke to anyone, "I was the first one here. I'm the one who rescued Hillary." The officer moves aside and Williams steps around him.

There on the basement floor is Zipper. Williams looks the scene over carefully. He wants to remember everything. He has a story to construct and he wants as many of the details to be as right as he can get them.

At the FHTF Situation Room, Admiral Baggott is speaking to the small assembled group- FBI Director Comey, White House Chief of Staff McNulty, Homeland Security Secretary Johnson, and Attorney General Michelle Obama, accompanied by four of her deputies and her five person security detail.

Mrs. Obama was appointed AG by her husband a month earlier, a "recess appointment" for the remainder of Obama's term, avoiding public hearings and Senate confirmation. In surprise televised remarks Obama compared himself to President John F. Kennedy who "more than fifty years ago, appointed his brother Robert to the same post. A magnificent choice, just like Michelle will prove to be."

Republicans, and even some Democrats, were furious, livid, friggin' beside themselves. Madder even when Michelle moved almost all of her 137 member personal staff from the White House to the DOJ. But all were aware of the immense popularity of Michelle as First Lady, a cultural celebrity seldom criticized and frequently drooled over by the press, African-Americans and liberal young women.

Opponents were privately sickened by the presumption and gall of Obama's appointment and Michelle's perceived authoritarian instincts, but were polite and restrained in their public comments, so enmeshed as they were in political correctness.

In a Gallup poll taken during Michelle's first week as AG, before she exercised any of the authority of the office, her popularity numbers plunged by ten per cent. She was liked and admired more when she was seen as a cheery, benign partner to the president rather than as the nation's top law officer.

The appointment of Michelle came in the immediate wake of the surprise resignation of Loretta Lynch Hargrove, the former New York City U.S. Attorney, who had been the first black woman (and the second woman after the hapless Janet Reno) to become U.S. Attorney General. Lynch was widely respected as a professional prosecutor despite some signs of partisan political activity in her past and the Senate confirmed her appointment.

She refused to offer the media a substantive set of reasons for leaving the post after just a year. Anonymous sources hinted to the New York Times that the decision was made to spend more time with her husband, Stephen Hargrove, who she had married at age 48 and whose health was thought to be fragile, though he was, in fact, still employed as a technician at the Showtime Cable TV network in New York.

But it was actually the thorough politicization of the DOJ under Holder, an unapologetic (and unadmitted) left-wing ideologue who brought in squads of radical-left lawyers to the federal payroll, many of them defenders of the captured jihadists at the Guantanamo Bay prison, men and women who as a group were totally unprofessional, that did Lynch in. Lynch found the DOJ hostile to the public interest and completely unmanageable after six years of Eric Holder.

"We just caught a message from the Chinese Ambassador to their Foreign Ministry. It essentially says that Hillary Clinton is safe and free. No other details." Baggott has no intention of sharing the code breaking of the Chinese Embassy or anything else from the decryption with

213

Michelle and her minions. He's already shared it with more people than he wanted to.

Denny Walsh, Assistant FBI director, head of the Criminal Division, bulls his way through the door. "Director Comey", he says. "Television news is reporting that Hillary has been found and she appears to be okay. The kidnappers are dead. Some D.C. cop shot them. She was in Georgetown all along."

"Oh, Hell," Kerry says out loud, thinking about the involvement of the Chinese, whatever that might amount to. "How am I going to deal with this?"

"You're not," Chief of Staff McNulty says, knowing that Kerry means the PRC and its Foreign Ministry. "You won't have to."

He turns to Michelle Obama and her entourage. He politely asks them to leave the room. The issue to be discussed does not involve any criminal matters and is on a need-to-know basis. Michelle and her crew leave to prepare for media interviews with chosen reporters, invariably minorities or female or both. McNulty wants the new AG gone because he cannot trust his boss's wife and her staff with what he is about to say. He dismisses the elderly stenographer as well, thanking her for her transcription, and she leaves.

"Gentlemen," he says, "What we've learned here about Chinese involvement stays here. Stays here forever. Under no circumstances at any time will anyone here talk about this. If the Chinese ever claim credit for this - and I think they won't - we will deny it.

"Hillary's kidnapping was an American problem. It will remain an American problem even if we did have some unacknowledged help in solving it and getting her back. We don't yet know who the two dead kidnappers are, whether there are others, or what their motives were. We will learn everything we can, obviously, and as quickly as possible. We don't know who killed the two kidnappers, either, but we do know that it was someone working at the direction of the PRC intelligence apparatus and the Chinese Embassy. We will likely never know for certain. We should just be happy that Mrs. Clinton is safe and has been found."

"The FBI will take the lead on the investigation. Director Comey has already sent a top squad of his agents to the house in Georgetown. He is getting the locals off the scene. Find out who the police were that got there first and isolate them. Get everyone else out of there. Whatever happened at that scene is about to become a Washington Police Department story, and we're going to write it. I know the rest of you, all of us, I suppose, would like some credit. But that's not in the cards."

McNulty continues, "There is something else, a serious unresolved problem.

"Let me relate a story. I think you will find in it an important historic parallel to our present problem with Mrs. Clinton. Important for our Democratic party, important for the morale of the people of this wonderful country, important for the public's continued trust in the seat of government.

"When I was young, I was friendly with a charming, older Washington attorney. Dead about ten years. I'm not going to mention his name. Some of you might have known him. He was in private practice but had spent his early years, in the 1950's through the mid 60's, at DOJ, much of the time in the Internal Security Division."

"One day at lunch, he and I happened to talk about the Eisenhower Administration's biggest scandal, when Ike's Chief of Staff took a fancy and expensive Vicuna fur overcoat and an oriental rug from a New England industrialist named Goldfine."

"The Chief of Staff was the former Republican governor of New Hampshire, Sherman Adams. He was one of the most powerful men in Washington then. You may remember the scandal."

"My friend was privy to the inside facts about the Adams/Goldfine case. He shared them with me. The most interesting part by far, which I had never heard before, or since, was about John McCormack, the Speaker of the House, an old time Democrat from Massachusetts. An icon to our party. A stern, penurious old guy. Never cheated on his wife; never flew in an airplane until he was 70 years old. Never missed a roll call. Ardent Catholic."

"Except," my friend told me "they found out that the Speaker was on the take. He had been given cash bribes by Goldfine, as bad or worse than Adams. The Speaker wasn't perfect after all; he had some larceny in his heart."

"So what did they do about it, you might ask? Nothing. The Speaker was allowed to go on with his life as a model American politician of impeccable integrity."

"My friend said that telling the American public that the Speaker was a crook, on top of the Adams scandal, would have been terrible for the country."

"I was really shocked," said McNulty. "I said to him, 'It would have been terrible for the Democrats, you mean."

"'Yes, that too,'" he agreed.

"He told me that the half dozen DOJ lawyers who knew, all young guys, took an oath to keep their mouths shut. The AG, who was a Republican, was never told. One of these young men then went to Boston by train on a weekend, took a taxi to the Speaker's old two-family house (a 'double decka' in localese) in West Roxbury and knocked on his door. The message to him was simple and clear. 'We know about Goldfine. We know everything. Stop, *now*. Never do this again - and we will keep it a secret for the sake of the country.'"

"McCormack said, 'Yes, I understand. Consider it done.' He was an old man, burdened by the knowledge of his sins, shamed to have others know as well. He had tears in his eyes. And that was it. Any questions?"

"Yes," says the FBI director. "Who among us will tell Hillary?"

"Do we have any volunteers?" asks McNulty, who looks around the room. There is silence.

"No?" he says. "Then I will do it myself." A few weeks later he did.

One by one, the men rise and leave. Secretary Kerry is last, shaking his head in disbelief as he walks out. It has been quite a day. The Chinese have done what we could not.

Within an hour, Officer Rodney Williams and two senior FBI agents are working out the details of his story. Williams was the only one on the scene when Hillary was found, so this would not be so difficult to do in the fog of confusion that had long ago settled over the case.

They will concoct a narrative of how Rodney had killed the kidnappers with an untraceable pistol Rodney had found in an alley after a robbery some years ago - the serial numbers had been burned off before he had found the Makarov, which oddly enough, seemed to have been fitted for a silencer, though none was ever found. B-Rod carried the Makarov in a holster on his ankle as a backup gun, a common practice for patrol officers. Rodney had always meant to turn in the gun to his patrol sergeant but eventually forgot about it. He had drawn it, rather than his Glock, because he had experienced a problem with a stiff trigger when he last fired the Glock at the police range.

The stunning fact is that he rescued Hillary all by himself. Everyone else arrived later. The hard part might be getting him to remember the details of whatever they put together. But, hey, practice makes perfect.

"Practice, practice, practice," the lead agent thinks to himself and strongly repeats to Rodney. "Repetition. That's the key."

Chapter Thirty-Five

Officer Rodney Williams, the 25-year police veteran, born and raised in the District by his loving and charming mom Stella, became the city's newest media celebrity – and very quickly is morphed by the media into an instant national hero and then an international celebrity.

The story of how Rodney B. Williams had become curious about the house at 3037 Dent Place, after seeing one of the occupants who didn't fit in with the neighborhood, how he had approached the house to ask questions, how he had knocked on the door only to have Wayne B. Wayne pull a gun on him when he opened it and saw a uniformed policeman, how he had outdrawn him and shot Wayne dead on the spot, how he had heard a woman's muffled cry downstairs, how he was certain it was Hillary, how he had rushed down the stairs, and how he had shot Billy Fly as he crossed the room presumably going for a gun, how he had found Hillary and brought her out to the front lawn while he called for backup assistance. No one ever asked about the bag of Chinese rice on the floor, thrown in the trash by one of the FBI agents.

The story was a sensation. Rodney B. Williams became a "True American Hero" and was referred to by that appellation in headlines around the world. Rodney's life became rosy.

Soon, he was presented the Presidential Medal of Freedom at the White House in front of a large, adoring crowd. The medallion was hung around his neck by the President, who called him "a hero for all ages." The award carried a special lifetime tax-free stipend of $50,000 a year (with a regular cost of living increase) voted to him by a grateful Congress. This would be added to the exceedingly generous D.C. Metropolitan Police Retirement and benefits, almost $100,000 a year - and, as the media frequently reminded the world, Rodney was only 46 years old.

Rodney, his mother Stella, and the two young Williams' girls were driven to the White House in the Second District's biggest SUV, lights flashing, siren blaring, in a motorcade led by PD motorcycles and the Chief herself, who thought as they approached the White House, old B-Rod has totally redeemed the Police Academy Class of 1989-90.

Captain Stacey Kiester-Garcia, still smarting from her Rodney-induced wound, was behind the wheel of the big SUV, ordered by Chief Lanier to drive Rodney and his family.

Meester Kiester held the car door open, after she drove in and parked under the portico at the West Wing. Rodney stepped onto the driveway as President Obama and Michelle came out to greet him, pumped his hand, squeezed his shoulder, and hugged Stella and the kids.

Within hours of their bodies being recovered and identified, Billy's and Wayne's identities were released to the public. The press turned their lives upside down, posthumously, but the only right wing tie they could find was Wayne's membership in the National Rifle Association. That was enough for some reporters.

Susan Sarandon, 70, the anti-gun activist, held a news conference at the National Press Club to demand that the leader of the NRA, Wayne LaPierre, apologize for the kidnapping of Hillary. She added that he should be indicted "for running a criminal enterprise."

Mr. La Pierre, in retaliation, called Sarandon "a wrinkled old gas bag" at his own Washington news conference. He ridiculed her political involvement, as a "liberal Christian," in the 2008 presidential campaign of the now disgraced John Edwards. When asked in New Hampshire, "What would Jesus do during this primary season?" she said, with a straight face, "I think Jesus would be very supportive of John Edwards."

To those oblivious of the good works of the Shriners, Wayne B. Wayne's membership as a Shriner and his fondness for wearing a red-tasseled fez around sick children in a local hospital smacked of pedophilia or at least of something sketchy and weird for a grown man. It helped tar him further in the press, even though he was already dead.

A Texas grand jury indicted the leader and two senior officers in Wayne's Frisco, Texas, Shriner's Lodge and charged them with conspiracy to commit a major felony - kidnapping. There wasn't a whit of direct evidence to support the charges, but a squad of Justice Department prosecutors, under the direct supervision of Attorney General Michelle Obama (who didn't like Hillary Clinton for certain but disliked white Texans even more) wove together a mass of circumstantial facts and passionate rhetoric. They were successful in getting a jury verdict against the "sinister trio of white men in their red bellboy hats," as an MSNBC reporter described the defendants.

Six months later, the three Shriners received life sentences with the possibility of parole after 20 years. All were men in their 50's. They obtained little sympathy outside of their families, neighbors and a few civil libertarians. They were dismissed as right-wingers by the media, although one was a Democrat and another hadn't voted in 30 years.

Earl "Fatha" Hines and Billy Crandall never told anyone of their involvement in the kidnapping and no one ever suspected.

In the fall of 2017, a year after Hillary's kidnapping, Earl accidently shot Billy while they were duck hunting - but not with a shotgun. The two had each drunk four cans of beer and were screwing around with Billy's Colt .45, Model 1911 - "one powerful MF," as Billy liked to say - which he frequently carried in a grizzled leather holster on his belt.

Billy handed the gun to Earl when he asked for it. Bad mistake.

Earl tried to shoot an approaching mallard with the .45. The plump male bird was 20 feet to port and slowly flaring for a landing in the water to the side of the blind when Earl whispered, "Watch this," and leaped up, cocking the pistol at the same moment that his feet slipped out from under him on the wet plywood flooring. He inadvertently squeezed the trigger. The gun was pointed down as he was falling and the bullet nailed Billy in the right thigh. The large slug passed through that leg, obliterated one testicle and emerged through the other side of his left leg.

Billy was rolling around, he was friggin' heavy, and Earl had a bitch of a time getting him out of the blind and then dragging him through two feet of water and weeds, with the dogs going crazy and jumping around, and Billy moaning in the most God-awful fashion, all the way to the damned truck.

He got him in the passenger seat and off they went towards the nearby town. As it turns out, Billy might have survived if Earl hadn't shortly run off the road into a drainage canal and drowned them both while rushing to the hospital. Their story disappeared with them. The two gun-dogs escaped injury and eventually wandered the five miles home to Earl's house.

Epilogue

Within two weeks of regaining her freedom, and after a surprise private visit to her home from the White House Chief of Staff Wallace McNulty, Hillary announced through a spokeswoman that she was dropping out of the race. She had been traumatized and exhausted by the kidnapping, she said in a statement.

Privately, she told friends that the lurid suggestions by some in the media that she had been sexually molested and abused bothered her, and were enervating, though she didn't illuminate them on the subject any further, leaving them guessing as to whether or not she had been. There were some real benefits to victimhood. Not having to explain yourself in detail was one of them.

The kidnappers had been actually respectful of her privacy and had treated her decently, though she didn't think it would be in her political interests to say so, or to say anything else about them, or what exactly happened to her at the hands of One and Two, and she never did, letting the false beliefs and rumors settle in to Public Conventional Wisdom.

The Washington Post, from which, in this case, the other major newspapers, and TV and radio, took their news cues, reported that she spent three months under the care of physicians, although she had not. A half-day was more like it. In fact, there were no doctors at all, except one the FBI brought in to examine her, and the tea she had at her house with a female psychiatrist, a friend and supporter (who she felt certain had never slept with Bill) who gave her soothing general counsel.

Word of her treatment by a psychiatrist was leaked purposefully by her minions, eliciting more sympathy and offering her further freedom from media harassment. She did do a few one-on-one puffball interviews with handpicked media sob sisters, including the lissome David Brock from Media Matters.

Hillary slept a lot (often with a soft smile on her face) in her huge house off Embassy Row in Washington, read the tabloids and newspapers, particularly about herself, and watched a lot of TV. She was a very rich woman. She had more than $100 million in assets, and that was separate from Bill, who had even more. She loved her few friends and her daughter and grandchildren, who sometimes visited from New York.

Huma Abedin, now 40-years-old, held her hand every day, even as they floated side-by-side, sometimes skinny-dipping in the heated backyard swimming pool, which was calming and luxurious.

Hillary had hand-washed her baseball PJ's and kept them folded, tucked away nicely in her lingerie drawer. For a while she had left them hanging in her bedroom closet in a plastic dry cleaning bag until Huma saw them and jokingly suggested a parallel with Monica Lewinsky's keeping her notorious black dress in a closet. Hillary didn't think that was particularly funny. The next day she moved the pajamas to her lingerie drawer. Once in a while, when she was alone, she wore them to bed.

She kept her Angelina Jolie mask wrapped in a pink, perfumed tea towel in a separate drawer. She had never shown it to anyone and wasn't actually sure why she had kept it. Although it was, of course, a souvenir of an intense and deeply emotional drama in her life, one, with its Chinese ramifications and the deaths of her kidnappers, that had changed her. But sometimes she would take it out and spread it on the pillow next to her when she was sleeping alone. She was not sure why and wasn't in the slightest tempted to ask the psychiatrist about it at tea.

She never did undergo detailed questioning about her time in captivity. Too delicate a subject, poor woman, God knows what was done to her, thought reporters. It was off-limits, in bad taste to ask, akin to media questions to Bill about Monica Lewinsky.

Hillary knew that she would have won the election hands down against any Republican if she had stayed in the race. Her role as a victim was too powerful in a society that had come to cherish and celebrate and reward the victimization of women. But the fires of ambition and insecurity that had burned within for so long were now dying. The fear of exposure over the Chinese money laundering, if she hadn't agreed to quit and retire from political life, was still alive.

There was a fierce floor flight at the Democratic Convention in Brooklyn in August. Joe Biden had jumped back in the race, as had others, some unexpected. Hillary Clinton stayed out of the donnybrook until the smoke settled. She then held a news conference in Washington to enthusiastically endorse the party nominee. It wasn't Joe.

Huma Abedin, and her 5-year old son Jordan, were now living at Whitehaven permanently. Huma had finally left her crazed husband, the former congressman Anthony Weiner, now a New York restaurant owner but still an overweening narcissist, after he was caught again in another "selfie" sex scandal. The man did have a sense of perverse humor. He had sent a picture of his fist wrapped around a king-sized kosher bratwurst (gluten and nitrate free) to a 22 year old Democrat party groupie named Wendy in Worthington, Ohio. He dubbed it in the email, "Weiner of the Month." Wendy's angry boyfriend sent it to columnist Andrea Payson at the New York Post. Payson ran a blistering piece touted on the Post front page above the color photo of the bratwurst with a banner that said, "THE WEINER IS BACK!"

On January 19, 2017, the day before the inauguration of the new President of the United States, Wallace McNulty

228

was headed back to his office from lunch. It would be his final day at the White House. A street vendor was selling toys from a van at the curb at H Street, around the corner from the august Metropolitan Club, a conservative stronghold. A small crowd was gathered.

A large white sign with red letters on the side of the van, said, "Celebrate Officer Rodney B. Williams Day, Feb. 16, 2017 – A People's Parade. Up Wisconsin Avenue in Georgetown. Commemorate the Shoot-Out and Rescue of Hillary Clinton by Officer B-Rod, our National Hero."

The Asian man was selling a "Mother Stella Doll" - a plump black woman in a red apron with a large submarine sandwich in her hand, at $9.95; an "Officer B-Rod doll" - a pudgy black man in a blue police uniform with a "genuine leather" ankle holster with a tiny pistol in it for $12.95; and the "Rescue Dolls" for $14.95 - B-Rod has his left arm protectively around a small blonde woman. She is pressed with her back against his chest ("They are sewn together forever, Mom, so they won't fall apart," says the tag.) Hillary is wearing plain pajamas (no one knew about the baseballs). Rodney has his right arm extended, gripping his pistol. The last item was a B-Rod Snack Pak Lunch Bucket made of tin with smiling giraffes on both sides, for $11.95

McNulty bought one of each, had them bagged, and said to the vendor, "Made in the US?"

"China," the man said.

McNulty walked down Pennsylvania Avenue to FBI headquarters. He left the bag for Director Comey with a note inside. It said, "Enjoy. Wallace."

At the Inauguration Ceremony, Rachel Maddow, 43, the openly gay former MSNBC TV anchor, looked splendiferous in a black Chesterfield coat with a velvet collar. She wore a dark blue men's pinstripe suit from J. Press in New Haven. A gray silk cravat was at her throat, held by a small gold stickpin. Tiny diamonds in its center spelled the word, "NOW."

Her black Homburg hat was identical to that worn by Dwight Eisenhower at his inaugural in 1953.

She stood straight and strong as she was sworn-in by Supreme Court Associate Justice Sonia Sottomayor as the 45th President of The United States.

The nation's new First Lady, blonde, plump Susan Mikula, the new president's mate of 17 years, leaned in next to her husband in the crisp winter wind, and squeezed her small hand.

Members of the DNC Women's Leadership Forum were seated en bloc nearby – Debbie Wasserman Schulz, Barbara Boxer, Maxine Waters, Elizabeth Warren, Jill Biden, Rosie O'Donnell, Nancy Pelosi, Carolyn Maloney, *et al*, each wearing a pink ribbon that stated, in blood red print, "NOW IS THE TIME!" It was President Maddow's campaign war-cry when she leaped into the race before the convention in Brooklyn, fueled by enormous financial support from George Soros and gay and lesbian organizations. She had beaten both Joe Biden and Andrew Cuomo in vicious floor fighting, walking away with the nomination and ultimately the Presidency.

Former Governor Mike Huckabee had quit his Fox TV and radio shows to run. The Real Man from Hope (unlike Bill Clinton, who was born in Hot Springs, Huckabee was born and raised in Hope, Arkansas) went on to win every state in the Republican primaries and then the nomination, facing off against Maddow.

Rand Paul, the Libertarian candidate, refused endless public (and many private) entreaties from conservatives to quit the race. He drew 16 per cent of the popular vote. Maddow beat Huckabee.

At the Tsin-Tsin cafe in Washington, Katie Wang sipped green tea and looked out the window. She smiled to herself as she listened to the inaugural on Chief's old radio in the kitchen.

Three months later, in a nonpareil historic event, former First Lady, former U.S. Senator and former Secretary of State Hillary Clinton was sworn in as an Associate Justice of the U.S. Supreme Court after appointment by President

Maddow and unanimous confirmation by a bipartisan
Senate.

THE END

About the Authors

Dick Carlson is a former U.S. Ambassador, the former Director of the Voice of America during the last six years of the Cold War, and a former President and CEO of the Corporation for Public Broadcasting. He was once a magazine writer and a television correspondent. He is co-host with Bill Cowan of the Danger Zone radio show. He lives with his wife Patricia in Washington, D.C.

Bill Cowan is a retired Marine Corps lieutenant colonel, highly decorated combat veteran with three purple hearts, and Fox News Channel military contributor. He spent most of his professional life engaged in special operations and activities in support of sensitive U.S. government programs abroad. A co-host of the Danger Zone radio show, he lives with his wife Velvet in Mt. Airy, North Carolina.

7/14

CPSIA information can be obtained at www.ICGtesting.com
Printed in the USA
LVOW04s1503180615

442982LV00019B/968/P